# Sacred Mountains

## Michael Berman

# Sacred Mountains
# Michael Berman

STORIES OF THE MYSTIC MOUNTAINS
AN ANTHOLOGY

## Mandrake

Copyright © 2013 Mandrake & Michael Berman
1st Edition

All rights reserved. No part of this work may be reproduced or utilized in any form by any means, electronic or mechanical, including *xerography, photocopying, microfilm*, and *recording*, or by any information storage system without permission in writing from the publishers.

Published by
Mandrake of Oxford
PO Box 250
OXFORD
OX1 1AP (UK)

# Contents

Introduction .................................................................................... 7
What are Mountains for you? ........................................................ 16
Soul Captivation on White Bone Mountain ................................ 30
The Magic Brush and the Golden Mountain ............................... 43
The Legend of Amirani ..................................................................
The Story of Jumping Mouse ........................................................ 68
The Children of Hamelin: A Shamanic Journey into Mount
Poppenberg ...................................................................................... 89
The Crystal Clear Waters of Mount Elbruz ................................ 110
The Vision Quest, Mount Sinai, and a Dream Fulfilled ............ 117
Mount Ararat ................................................................................. 135
Mount Koya-san, the Hermit's Cave, and Fujiyama
Sacred Towers ............................................................................... 154
The Fool on the Hill and the Book of Mysteries ....................... 168
The Tobacco of Harisaboqued ..................................................... 180
The Princess of the Tower ............................................................ 183

Appendix:
The Baal Shem Tov –
Rabbi, Religious Formulator or Shaman? ................................... 197

**Monument to Garegin Njdeh and Mount Khustup**

# Introduction

All the stories presented in this collection contain shamanic elements, so the obvious starting point is to explain what is meant by this. The term 'shaman' is a controversial one. Initially employed by early anthropologists to refer to a specific category of magical practitioners from Siberia, the term is now widely used to denote similar practitioners from a variety of cultures around the world. This application of an originally culture-specific term to a more general usage has caused problems with regard to definition, with disagreements among scholars over whether certain features, such as soul flight or possession, or certain types of altered states of consciousness, should or should not be listed among the core characteristics of shamanism (Wilby, 2011, p.252).

As a result, there are as many definitions of shamanism as there are books written on the subject. Here is my version:

A shaman is someone who performs an ecstatic (in a trance state), imitative, or demonstrative ritual of a séance (or a combination of all three), at will (in other words, whenever he or she chooses to do so), in which aid is sought from beings in (what are considered to be) other realities generally for healing purposes or for divination–both for individuals and / or the community.

For the shaman, the structure of the cosmos is frequently symbolized by the number seven, made up of the four directions, the centre, the zenith in heaven, and the nadir in the Underworld. The essential axes of this structure are the four cardinal points and a central vertical axis passing through their point of intersection that connects the Upper World, the Middle World and the Lower World. The names by which the central vertical axis that connects the three worlds is referred to, include the world pole, the tree of life, the sacred mountain, the central house pole, and Jacob's ladder. So important is this cosmology considered to be that religion itself has been described by Berger (1969) as the enterprise we undertake to establish just such a sacred cosmos.

Different types of shamanic journeys can be undertaken–to the Lower World where you can make contact with Power Animals and to the Upper World where you can meet your Sacred Teacher.[1]

The starting point for a journey to the Upper World can be a mountain, a treetop, or even a ladder, from which the shaman envisions himself ascending into the sky; "and despite the variety of socio-religious contexts in which it occurs, the ascent always has the same goal–meeting with the Gods or heavenly powers, in order to obtain a blessing (whether a personal consecration, a favour for the community, or the cure of a sick person)" (Eliade, 1958, p.77). At some stage of the journey the shaman may come up against a kind of barrier that temporarily impedes the ascent. But once this has been successfully negotiated, the Upper World is reached.

Journeys are also undertaken to the Land of the Dead, where the shaman acts as a psychopomp – a conductor of souls. Sometimes the Land of the Dead is antipodal, meaning everything there is reversed: day here is night there, and vice versa. There are journeys

---

1   "While it is true that man depends on his Gods, the dependence is mutual. The Gods also need man, without offerings and sacrifices, they would die" (Durkheim, 2001, p.38)

   This applies equally well to the Sacred Teachers and Power Animals met by shamanic practitioners on their journeys to other realities. This is why the shaman is required to both respect and honour these Helpers who assist him or else they will desert him.

for the purpose of divination and journeys to carry out Soul Retrievals too. Soul loss is the term used to describe the way parts of the psyche become detached when we are faced with traumatic situations. In psychological terms, it is known as dissociation and it works as a defence mechanism, a means of displacing unpleasant feelings, impulses or thoughts into the unconscious. In shamanic terms, these split-off parts can be found in non-ordinary reality and are only accessible to those familiar with its topography (see Gagan, 1998, p.9).

Sandra Ingerman, a neo-shamanic practitioner who specialises in soul retrievals and has written several books that deal with the subject, believes that sometimes the soul is afraid to come back, especially if it is a part that was abused at an early age. Soul theft is also a possibility—another person taking a piece of our essence so they can cling to us, or to steal our power or energy (see Ingerman, 1993, p.26).

As for Middle-World journeys, accounts of these have been recorded in areas where food supplies are precarious and migrating animal herds must be located such as in the near-Arctic areas of North America and Siberia.

On neo-shamanic workshops such as those taught by Michael Harner (The Foundation for Shamanic Studies) or Jonathan Horwitz (the Scandinavian Center for Shamanic Studies), participants are taught how to journey to the Middle World to see events that take place in this reality in their non-ordinary reality forms and to gain a greater insight into their nature. But what is this other dimension of our world like and how can it be described to someone who has never experienced it? As has already been pointed out, for each person who "journeys" the experience is unique so generalisation cannot be particularly accurate. However, this is what Ingerman has to say about it:

> In non-ordinary reality, the Middle World comes closest to our ordinary reality. Here I see scenes that I would experience in my waking life, but I am in an altered state of consciousness when looking at them. ... Shamans usually travel to the Middle World to find lost and stolen objects. I also travel to the Middle World to speak to the spirit of a client who is in a coma or unconscious to get permission to do healing work on his or her behalf (Ingerman, 1993, p.172).

How can these other worlds be accessed? The journey frequently involves passing through some kind of gateway. As Eliade explains,

> The 'clashing of rocks,' the 'dancing reeds,' the 'gates in the shape of jaws,' the 'two razor-edged restless mountains,' the 'two clashing icebergs,' the 'active door,' the 'revolving barrier,' the 'door made of the two halves of the eagle's beak,' and many more – all these are images used in myths and sagas to suggest the insurmountable difficulties of passage to the Other World (Eliade, 2003, pp.64-65).

And to make such a journey requires a change in one's mode of being, entering a transcendent state, which makes it possible to attain the world of spirit.

> Ascent and flight are proofs par excellence of the divinization of man. The specialists in the sacred – medicine men, shamans, mystics – are above all men who are believed to fly up to Heaven, in ecstasy or even in the flesh ... The descent to the Underworld and the ascent to

Heaven obviously denote different religious experiences; but the two experiences spectacularly prove that he who has undergone them has transcended the secular condition of humanity and that his behaviour is purely that of a spirit (Eliade, 2003, p.78).

Eliade paints a picture of the shaman here that could well have the effect of being disempowering as it makes the rest of us feel somewhat inferior to such gifted people and results in us treating them with perhaps excessive reverence. On the other hand, neo-shamanic workshop facilitators such as Harner and Horwitz, train participants to become their own shamans and thus see what they do as a form of empowerment.

Indigenous peoples who have lost their traditions over the course of time are now turning to, or being assisted by neo-shamanic practitioners, to rediscover their roots and to reactivate their traditions. In present-day Armenia, for example, healing traditions have been revitalized since the country regained its independence from the Soviet Union.

Some theories state that periods of crisis impact the growth and energetic potential of a society and engender a strong need for ancient rehabilitation mechanisms such as shamanism or similar practices (Kharitonova, 1999, p.53) This theory seems to hold in the case of Armenia, the world's oldest Christian culture, where many components of traditional shamanistic practices are alive and flourishing (Antonian, 2003, p.51).

Not only are they flourishing, but as Antonian (2009) points out, interesting new developments can be observed to be taking place now too.

Unlike the first members of the neo-pagan community, who

were mainly attracted by nationalist approaches and the romanticism of old Armenian beliefs, more recent adherents have accepted paganism for mystic reasons. They began believing in ancient Gods, because they have got mystical help from them.

On reading this, I contacted Antonian to find out exactly what she meant by "mystical", thinking it might have been a mistranslation, and this was her reply:

Regarding your question, I meant people have started having visions, dreams about the Ancient Gods, and I came across some very interesting examples of this - very close to what can be described as shamanic ones. A man who calls himself an "epic singer" ("Ashugh") said that his songs were inspired by the Ancient Gods he was having visions of. Some of them even confessed that they had been converted to paganism, following their prayers, as the Gods had given them what they wanted (e.g. kids). The number of such people is not too large yet, however there are others who keep trying to have some mystical experiences too. For instance, every year a certain number of "arordis" (this is what neo-pagans call themselves) climb Mount Khustup to spend a night there in the hope of having a vision of Vahagn, one of the most important deities in the Armenian pagan pantheon\*. This is exactly what I mean by saying "mystic" and "spiritual" (personal correspondence received 22/11/09).

As for the significance of Mount Khustup,

the Arordis believe (or pretend to believe) it was on this

particular mountain in 1921, when Nzhdeh was defending Syunik region (in the South of Armenia) from the Turks and Azeris, that he had a vision of Vahagn, who gave him the idea for his spiritual mission. So, spending a night at the top of Mount Khustup is about following in the footsteps of Nzhdeh, who plays a role close to that one Christ plays in Christianity. Climbing Khustup is not just about getting closer to the centre of the Universe but also a ritual reiteration of the First Contact with the Ancient Gods experienced by someone who is regarded as a "messiah" by his adherents (ibid).

So although the neo-pagan movement in Armenia was initially little more than a means of expressing the ethnic nationalism of the people, a reaction against the situation they found themselves in during Soviet times, it would now seem to be developing into something quite different.

The journeys that the stories in *Sacred Mountains* are accounts of are all to the Upper World, taken from a variety of different cultures, and it is hoped that you will find the material both informative and enlightening.

# References

Antonian, Y. (2003) 'Pre-Christian Healers in a Christian Society' In *Cultural Survival Quarterly* Summer 2003.

Antonian, Y. (2008) 'Magical and healing practices in a contemporary urban environment (in the Armenian cities of Yerevan, Gyumri, and Vanadzor)' In *Figuring the South Caucasus: Societies and Environment – A Collection of papers on Sociology, Political Studies, Anthropology and Gender studies*, Tbilisi: Heinrich Böll Foundation.

Antonian, Y. (2009) "Re-creation" of a religion: neo-paganism in Armenia [The draft of a Paper to be published in *Laboratorium*, Saint-Petersburg] http://yerevan.academia.edu/YuliaAntonyan/Papers [accessed 20/11/09].

Berger, P. (1973) *The Social Reality of Religion*, Harmondsworth: Penguin

Couliano, I.P. (1991) *Out of this World*, Boston: Shambhala.

Dioszegi, V. (1968) *Tracing Shamans in Siberia: The Story of an Ethnographical Research Expedition*, Oosterhout: Anthropological Publications.

Durkheim, E. (2001) *The Elementary Forms of Religious Life*, Oxford: Oxford University Press (originally published in 1912).

Eliade, M. (1957) *The Sacred and the Profane: The Nature of Religion*, New York: Harper & Row.

—. (1989) *Shamanism: Archaic techniques of ecstasy*, London: Arkana (first published in the USA by Pantheon Books 1964).

—. (2003) *Rites and Symbols of Initiation*, Putnam, Connecticut: Spring Publications (originally published by Harper Bros., New York, 1958).

Gagan, J.M. (1998) *Journeying: where shamanism and psychology meet*, Santa Fe, NM: Rio Chama Publications.

Ingermann, S. (1991) *Soul Retrieval: Mending the Fragmented Self through Shamanic Practice*, San Francisco: Harper.

—. (1993) *Welcome Home: Following Your Soul's Journey Home*, New York: Harper Collins Publishers.

Kharitonova, V. (1999) *Spelling-conjuring art of the East Slavs: Problems of traditional interpretations and possibilities of modern research*. Moscow, Russia: Institute of Ethnology and Anthropology of Russian Academy of Sciences.

Wilby, E. (2011) *The Visions of Isobel Gowdie: Magic, Witchcraft and Dark Shamanism in Seventeenth-Century Scotland*, Eastbourne: Sussex Academic Press.

# 1
# What are Mountains for you?

Come Fairies, take me out of this dull world, for I would ride with you upon the wind and dance upon the mountains like a flame!
~ William Butler Yeats

My father considered a walk among the mountains as the equivalent of churchgoing. ~ Aldous Huxley

It does not matter how slow you go, as long as you don't stop.
~ Confucius

Short is the little time which remains to thee of life. Live as on a mountain. ~ Marcus Aurelius, *Meditations*

Men go abroad to wonder at the heights of mountains, at the huge waves of the sea, at the long courses of the rivers, at the vast compass of the ocean, at the circular motions of the stars, and they pass by themselves without wondering. ~ Saint Augustine

He who climbs upon the highest mountains laughs at all tragedies, real or imaginary. ~ Friedrich Nietzsche, *Thus Spake Zarathustra*

What is straight? A line can be straight, or a street, but the human

heart, oh, no, it's curved like a road through mountains.
~ Tennessee Williams

We sit together, the mountain and me, until only the mountain remains. ~ Li Po

Mountain, thou art always the refuge of the good who practise the law of righteousness, the hermits of holy deeds who seek out the road that leads to heaven. It is by thy grace, Mountain, that priests, warriors and commoners attain to heaven and, devoid of pain, walk with the Gods. ~ *The Mahabharata*

There are some moments like walking in the mountains after the rain when you feel it is so wonderful to be human. ~ Shen Wei

Great things are done when men and mountains meet. This is not done by jostling in the street. ~ William Blake

When he took time to help the man up the mountain, lo, he scaled it himself. ~ Tibetan Proverb

For a short time we lived quietly. But this could not last. White men had found gold in the mountains around the land of winding water.
~ Chief Joseph

On the mountains of truth you can never climb in vain: either you will reach a point higher up today, or you will be training your powers so that you will be able to climb higher tomorrow.
~ Friedrich Nietzsche

It isn't the mountains ahead to climb that wear you out; it's the pebble in your shoe. ~ Muhammad Ali

Mountains are earth's undecaying monuments.
~ Nathaniel Hawthorne (American short-story writer and novelist, master of the allegorical and symbolic tale. 1804-1864)

Mountains are the beginning and the end of all natural scenery.
~ John Ruskin

Now suddenly there was nothing but a world of cloud, and we three were there alone in the middle of a great white plain with snowy hills and mountains staring at us; and it was very still; but there were whispers. ~ Black Elk

The colour of the mountains is Buddha's body; the sound of running water is his great speech. ~ Dogen

How beautiful on the mountains are the feet of those who bring good news, who proclaim peace, who bring good tidings.
~ Bible quotes

In the mythic tradition, the Mountain is the bond between Earth and Sky. Its solitary summit reaches the sphere of eternity, and its base spreads out in manifold foothills into the world of mortals. It is the way by which man can raise himself to the divine and by which the divine can reveal itself to man.
~ René Daumal, *Mount Analogue*

On every mountain height is rest.
~ Johann Wolfgang von Goethe, *Ein Gleiches*

A proud heart and a lofty mountain are never fruitful.
~ George Eliot (pseudonym of Mary Ann Evans Cross)

And o'er the hills and far away, Beyond their utmost purple rim, Beyond the night, across the day, Thro' all the world she followed him. ~ Lord Alfred Tennyson

The Beauty of the Mountain is hidden for all those who try to discover it from the top, supposing that, one way or another, one can reach this place directly. The Beauty of the Mountain reveals only to those who climbed it. ~ Antoine de Saint-Exupéry

Come live with me, and be my love, And we will all the pleasures prove, That valleys, groves, hills, and fields, Woods, or steepy mountains yields. ~ Christopher Marlowe

Never measure the height of a mountain, until you have reached the top. Then you will see how low it was.
~ Dag Hammarskjöld

In the mountains, the shortest way is from peak to peak: but for that you must have long legs
~ Friedrich Nietzsche
(German classical Scholar, Philosopher and Critic of culture, 1844-1900.)

Round its breast the rolling clouds are spread,
Eternal sunshine settles on its head.
~ Oliver Goldsmith, *The Deserted Village* (l. 192)


I am here for a purpose and that purpose is to grow into a mountain, not to shrink to a grain of sand. Henceforth will I apply ALL my efforts to become the highest mountain of all and I will strain my potential until it cries for mercy.
~ Og Mandino
(American Essayist and Psychologist, 1923-1996)
Above me are the Alps,

The palaces of Nature, whose vast walls
Have pinnacled in clouds their snowy scalps,
And thron'd Eternity in icy halls
Of cold sublimity, where forms and falls
The avalanche—the thunderbolt of snow!
All that expands the spirit, yet appals,
Gather round these summits, as to show
How Earth may pierce to Heaven, yet leave vain man below.
~ Lord Byron (George Gordon Noel Byron)


If you wait for the perfect moment when all is safe and assured, it may never arrive. Mountains will not be climbed, races won, or lasting happiness achieved.
~ Maurice Chevalier

What will this boaster produce worthy of this mouthing? The mountains are in labor; a ridiculous mouse will be born.
~ Quintus Horatius Flaccus

Study how water flows in a valley stream, smoothly and freely between the rocks. Also learn from holy books and wise people. Everything - even mountains, rivers, plants and trees - should be your teacher.
~ Morihei Ueshiba

They that stand high have many blasts to shake them; And if they fall they dash themselves to pieces.
~ William Shakespeare *Richard III*

Nobody climbs mountains for scientific reasons. Science is used to raise money for the expeditions, but you really climb for the hell of it.
~ Edmund Hillary
(New Zealander mountain climber and Antarctic Explorer. Famous for being first to successfully climb Mount Everest)

May your trails be crooked, winding, lonesome, dangerous, leading to the most amazing view. May your mountains rise into and above the clouds. ~ Edward Abbey

We can scale the heights of mountains and see the world rayed out before us, but we fail to recognize that which is before us.
~ Ruth St.Denis (a modern dance pioneer)

You cannot stay on the summit forever; you have to come down again. So why bother in the first place? Just this: What is above knows what is below, but what is below does not know what is above. One climbs, one sees. One descends, one sees no longer, but one has seen. There is an art of conducting oneself in the lower regions by the memory of what one saw higher up. When one can no longer see, one can at least still know. ~ René Daumal

I experienced a feeling of total connection with the landscape and a sense of deep security while travelling through the Andes on the narrow gauge railway from Cusco to Machu Picchu. I became the mountain and a sort of benevolence flowed into me. It was the strongest feeling of peace I have ever had, despite the fact that mudslides had devastated villages the week before taking many lives. Bizarrely, at the same time a fashion show was taking place up and down the length of the train, the ticket collectors had donned Peruvian knitwear and were sweeping down the aisles posturing and taking orders adding a surreal aspect to my all-encompassing bliss. Paradoxical!
~ Angela Davis http://www.artshamanic.com

My souvenir from Edo
Is the refreshingly cold wind
Of Mount Fuji
I brought home on my fan.
~ Matsuo Basho, 1676

Encountering the sacred in mountain landscapes is as much a pilgrimage as any other journey of devotion and quest. The ascent of a mountain face or path can symbolize a search for fresh insights

and understanding of ourselves and of the world in which we live.
~ Adrian Cooper (writer and broadcaster)

As the mountains surround Jerusalem, so the Lord surrounds his people both now and forevermore. (Taken from *Psalm* 125)

> Mountains!
> You pierce the blue sky,
> without blunting your peaks.
> But for your support
> Heaven would fall.     ~ Mao Tse Tung, 1976

From time immemorial the mountains have been the dwelling place of the great sages; wise men and sages have all made the mountains their own chambers, their own body and mind.
~ Dogen, *Treasury of the True Dharma Eye: Book* XXIX, The Mountains and Rivers Sutra

If among the objects of the world of spirit there is something fixed and unalterable, great and illimitable, something from which the beams of revelation, the streams of knowledge, pour into the mind like water into a valley, it is to be symbolized by a mountain.
~ Al-Ghazali (Islamic Sufi mystic)

The symbolic and religious significance of mountains is endless.
~ Mircea Eliade, in *Patterns in Comparative Religion*

If you climb Mount T'ai [T'ai Shan Eastern China], you may see the immortal beings. They feed on the purest jade, they drink from

the springs of manna. They yoke the scaly dragons to their carriage, they mount the floating clouds.
~ Emperor Wu-ti, Han dynasty.

Brooding over some vast mountain landscape, or among the spiritual countenances of mountain flowers, our bodies disappear, our mortal coils come off without any shuffling, and we blend into the rest of Nature, utterly blind to the boundaries that measure human qualities into separate individuals.
~ John Muir (American naturalist, and author)

What I have learned from my journey to the sacred mountain, and must now try to put into practice, is that instead of busying myself putting others down, which is what I have tended to do in the past, my time would be better spent helping those I criticise to rise up with me instead - that this is the secret to touching those I meet with goodness, and that this way we can live on in people's memories, long after we leave this world, whether we are blessed with children of our own or not. This way we can all leave a mark.
~ Michael Berman

For me, personally, the major motive for being on a mountain path has always been to locate the exact place where three countries meet. Not all such tripoints, of course, are in mountainous districts – they can also be in rivers or in lakes, in fact almost anywhere. There is one particular thing with mountains, however, that astonishes me. Whenever I reach a tripoint high up in the mountains, I do not, despite my reason for being there, get most of the satisfaction from being able to tick off yet another item on my visiting list. The ultimate

pleasure comes from the feeling of being so very small in such a vast, undisturbed, natural environment. Extra spices are surprisingly often added without previous warning, like the ones provided by heavy rain, black clouds and colourful flashes of lightning in the Sesvenna Range of the Swiss Alps a couple of years ago. We were enjoying coffee at the Austrian-Italian-Swiss tripoint some 800 metres north of the summit of Piz Lad when, in almost no time at all, there was a powerful thunderstorm. The sky suddenly got very dark although most of the clouds were virtually below us, and I felt so extremely tiny and helpless indeed - yet at the same so very close to our creator.
~ Rolf Palmberg - http://www.vasa.abo.fi/users/rpalmber/

What mountains mean to me: in one word, aweinspiring. Although we can measure them, our minds are incapable of actually grasping the very small or the very large things in nature: neither atomic particles nor astronomical distances. How big is a mountain, how much does it weigh? Our limited minds can only cope with subjective assessments such as how difficult is it to climb, how dangerous would an avalanche be? So the feelings it produces are awe, a little fear, and possibly exhilaration if and when we think that we have conquered the mountain – but in reality we never can.
~ Professor David Hunt
(formerly of London Southbank University, also folklorist and translator)

"Because it is there" ... is a convenient start but an unsatisfactory conclusion. The human condition spreads to fill the universal void. The animal kingdom is bound by its limitations but we humans can control all that. Nothing stops us. How we managed to populate each 'nook and cranny' and survive to evolve racial characteristics is something to marvel at — the forbidden depths, the frozen wastes the searing sun and empty space.

So what about Mountains? The crags, the cliffs, inaccessibility to the Urban pedestrian leaves him in fear and wonder to create myths and legends.

The Mountaineers (and I) know this territory. We have the skills to move and survive on the precipitous rockface — to know what is possible. My mind is focussed upon feasibility. I calculate the probability of progress from distance, surface contour and roughness and compile a route. The climb begins and each move translates my calculations into balance and posture. The eyes focus upon features the fingers and feet feel security. The time comes to belay and secure the ropes so others can follow.

The concentration required blocks out the distraction, but upon reaching safety, the opportunity to open the senses (and the 'heart and soul') to the scale and grandeur, the height and the depth the expansive and expanding distant horizon. A transcendental experience fills the 'soul'. Although a sense of affinity with nature prevails there is the understanding that we are not part of the environment, and as I grow older and less capable, I become more aware of this.

Afterwards, in the domestic warmth of a welcome pub, the day is relived, the adventures recalled. Singing songs and playing tunes in the company of like minds celebrates the communion with the mountains.

~ Dave Ellis (folksinger and mountaineer)

My favourite mountain, if you can call it that, is the Tor in Somerset in Glastonbury. Years ago, the second time I went there, we passed it in the car and I heard the most amazing music. Can't describe how beautiful it was. When I asked which channel to the driver she showed me that there was no radio-cassette or CD player in the car at all! Later that afternoon, sitting in the Courtyard, some locals overheard me talking about this. They smiled and said that I was welcomed by the music of the Fairy Court of Gwyn App Nudd, the Lord of the Underworld who resides in the Tor. They said: "The Fey Folk certainly like you!" I know this might sound a bit strange but the music was truly out of this World!

The very next day was for a Grand Ritual on an autumn morning, to watch the sunrise with a like-minded group together. We had to get up at 4 in the early hours of the morning and, climbing in the cold and the appropriate mists surrounding the Tor, it felt magical. At the top after listening to the Evocations, I uttered the words to The Lord of this realm and sighed: "Oh, I wish I could live here one day!" And exactly 10 years later I did - unexpectedly! The first thing I did was pour a libation to him and his Fey Court.

During my lovely 7 years living in Glastonbury with my children, the most wondrous events where I was present and stories came from the Tor visitors. Some people literally could not climb up, as if they were held back by an invisible barrier. Seeing their friends moving closer to the top, they had to sit it out! Or some, waking up in the middle of the night, felt a push to climb up there! Others were blown off the Tor while there was no wind at all. Luckily they didn't get hurt. Most locals didn't go near the Tor and certainly not to the top! When I asked why they replied that they were afraid of the Lord of the Underworld.

On the millennium evening almost the whole town went drumming to the Tor, and it was lit by thousands of candles around the platform, an amazing sight!

This all sounds like a Magical Fairy tale, but if you are nearby, climb to the top and feel the atmosphere for yourself. Look at the view; it is truly breath taking.

There are many stories about Mountains but when I was a child one of my favourite stories was, and still is, *The Glass Mountain*. The hero of the story, dressed in golden armour, has to go up a glass mountain to find the princess. Eventually, after numerous failed attempts, he manages to get halfway up, only to find a catlike creature that attacks him. Appropriating its claws, he fixes them to his own hands and feet, and then uses them to help him climb up to the top. A dragon awaits him there. While struggling with it, he notices an Apple tree; he throws an Apple to the mighty dragon and it disappears. His princess is in the Tower; they fall in love, he frees her, and together they slide off the Glass Mountain and ride to the palace to be wedded at sunset.

The fun thing of it all is that The Tor is also called Ynys Witrin, or "Glass Isle", with a Tower on the top, and an apple is the "key" that is needed to meet the Fey Folk!

~ Marielle Holman,

(Yoga teacher, Reiki practitioner, and storyteller)

**White Bone Mountain**

# 2
# Soul Captivation on White Bone Mountain

At the foot of Mount Shumongatake, up in the northwestern province of Echigo, once stood, and probably even still stands in rotten or repaired state, a temple of some importance, inasmuch as it was the burial-ground of the feudal Lord Yamana's ancestors. The name of the temple was Fumonji, and many high and important priests kept it up generation after generation, owing to the early help received from Lord Yamana's relations. Among the priests who presided over this temple was one named Ajari Joan, who was the adopted son of the Otomo family.

Ajari was learned and virtuous, and had many followers; but one day the sight of a most attractive girl called Kiku,* whose age was eighteen, upset all his religious equilibrium. He fell desperately in love with her, offering to sacrifice his position and reputation if she would only listen to his prayer and marry him; but the lovely O Kiku San refused all his entreaties. A year later she was taken seriously ill with fever and died, and whispers went abroad that Ajari the priest had cursed her in his jealousy and brought about her illness and her

---

\* Chrysanthemum.

death. The rumour was not exactly without reason, for Ajari went mad within a week of O Kiku's death. He neglected his services, and then got worse, running wildly about the temple, shrieking at night and frightening all those who came near. Finally, one night he dug up the body of O Kiku and ate part of her flesh.

People declared that he had turned into the Devil, and none dared go near the temple; even the younger priests left, until at last he was alone. So terrified were the people, none approached the temple, which soon ran to rack and ruin. Thorny bushes grew on the roof, moss on the hitherto polished and matted floors; birds built their nests inside, perched on the mortuary tablets, and made a mess of everything; the temple, which had once been a masterpiece of beauty, became a rotting ruin.

One summer evening, some six or seven months later, an old woman who owned a tea-house at the foot of Shumongatake Mountain was about to close her shutters when she was terrified at the sight of a priest with a white cap on his head approaching. "The Devil Priest! The Devil Priest!" She cried as she slammed the last shutter in his face. "Get away, get away! We can't have you here."

"What do you mean by 'Devil Priest'? I am a travelling or pilgrim priest, not a robber. Let me in at once, for I want both rest and refreshment," cried the voice from outside. The old woman looked through a crack in the shutters, and saw that it was not the dreaded maniac, but a venerable pilgrim priest: so she opened the door and let him in, profuse in her apologies, and telling him how they were all frightened out of their wits by the priest of Fumonji Temple who had gone mad over a love-affair.

"Oh, sir, it is truly terrible! We hardly dare go within half a mile of the temple now, and some day the mad priest is sure to come out of it and kill some of us."

"Do you mean to tell me that a priest has so far forgotten himself as to break through the teachings of Buddha and make himself the slave of worldly passions?" asked the traveller.

"I don't know about the worldly passions," cried the old lady; "but our priest has turned into a devil, as all the people hereabouts will tell you, for he has even dug up and eaten of the flesh of the poor girl whom he caused to die by his cursing!"

"There have been instances of people turning devils,' said the priest; 'but they are usually common people and not priests. A courtier of the Emperor So's turned into a serpent, the wife of Yosei into a moth, the mother of Ogan into a Yasha;* but I have never heard of a priest turning into a devil. Besides, Ajari Joan, your priest at Fumonji Temple, was a virtuous and clever man, I have always heard. I have come here, in fact, to do myself the honour of meeting him, and to-morrow I shall go and see him."

The old lady served the priest with tea and begged him to think of no such thing; but he persisted, and said that on the morrow he would do as he mentioned, and read the mad priest a lecture; and then he laid himself down to rest for the night.

Next afternoon the old priest, true to his word, started for the Fumonji Temple, the old lady accompanying him for the first part of the walk, to the place where the path which led to the temple turned up the mountain, and there she bade him good-bye, refusing to go another step.

The sun was beginning to set as the priest came in sight of the

---

\* Vampire bat.

temple, and he saw that the place was in great disorder. The gates had tumbled off their hinges, withered leaves were thickly strewn everywhere and crumpled under his feet; but he walked boldly on, and struck a small temple-bell with his staff. At the sound came many birds and bats from the temple, the bats flapping round his head; but there was no other sign of life. He struck the bell again with renewed force, and it boomed and clanged in echoes. At last a thin, miserable-looking priest came out, and, looking wildly about, said:

"Who are you, and why have you come here? The temple has long since been deserted, for some reason which I cannot understand. If you want lodging you must go to the village. There is neither food nor bedding here."

"I am a priest from Wakasa Province. The pretty scenery and clear streams have caused me to linger long on my journey. It is too late now to go to the village, and I am too tired: so please let me remain for the night," said the priest. The other made answer:

"I cannot order you away. This place is no longer more than a ruined shed. You can stay if you like; but you can have neither food nor bedding." Having said this, he sat on the corner of a rock, while the pilgrim priest sat on another, close by. Neither spoke until it was dark and the moon had risen. Then the mad priest said, "Find what place you can inside to sleep. There are no beds; but what there is of the roof keeps the mountain dew from falling on you during the night, and it falls heavily here and wets you through." Then he went into the temple—the pilgrim priest could not tell where, for it was dark and he could not follow, the place being littered with idols and beams and furniture which the mad priest had hacked to pieces in the early stages of his madness. The pilgrim, therefore, felt his way about until he found himself between a large fallen idol and a wall; and here he decided to spend the night, it being as safe a place in which to hide from the maniac as any he could find without knowing his way about or having a light. Fortunately for himself, he was a strong and healthy old man and was well able to do without food, and also to stand unharmed the piercing and damp cold. The pilgrim priest could hear the sound of the many streams which gurgled down the mountain-side. There was also the unpleasant sound of squeaking rats as they chased and fought, and of bats which flew in and out of the place, and of hooting owls; but beyond this nothing—nothing of the mad priest. Hour after hour passed thus until one o'clock, when suddenly, just as the pilgrim felt himself dozing off, he was aroused by a noise. The whole temple seemed as if it were being knocked down. Shutters were slammed with such violence that they fell to the floor; right and left idols and furniture were being hurled about. In and out ran the sound of the naked pattering feet of the crazed priest, who shouted:

"Oh, where is the beautiful O Kiku, my sweetly beloved Kiku? Oh, where, oh, where is she? The gods and the devils have combined to defraud me of her, and I care for neither and defy them all. Kiku, Kiku, come to me!"

The pilgrim, thinking his cramped position would be dangerous if the maniac came near him, availed himself of an opportunity, when the latter was in a far-off part of the temple, to get out into the grounds and hide himself again. It would be easier to see what went on, thought he, and to run if necessary.

He hid himself first in one part of the grounds and then in another. Meanwhile the mad priest paid several rushing visits to the outsides of the temple, keeping up all the time his awful cries for O

Kiku. Towards morning he retired once more to the part of the temple in which he lived, and no more noise was made. Our pilgrim then went forth from his hiding, and seated himself on the rock which he had occupied the evening before, determined to see if he could not force a conversation with the demented man and read him a lesson from the sacred teachings of Buddha. He sat patiently on until the sun was high; but all remained silent. There was no sign of the mad priest.

Towards midday the pilgrim heard sounds in the temple; and by and by the madman came out, looking as if he had just recovered from a drunken orgy. He appeared dazed and was quiet, and started as he saw the old priest seated on the rock as he had been the night before. The old man rose, and approaching him said:

"My friend, my name is Ungai. I am a brother priest—from the Temple of Daigoji, in Wakasa Province. I came hither to see you, hearing of your great wisdom; but last night I heard in the village that you had broken your vows as a priest and lost your heart to a maiden, and that from love of her you have turned into a dangerous demon. I have in consequence considered it my duty to come and read you a lecture, as it is impossible to pass your conduct unnoticed. Pray listen to the lecture and tell me if I can help you."

The mad priest answered quite meekly:

"You are indeed a Buddha. Please tell me what I can do to forget the past, and to become a holy and virtuous priest once more."

Ungai answered:

"Come out here into the grounds and seat yourself on this rock." Then he read a lecture out of the Buddhist Bible, and finished by saying, "And now, if you wish to redeem your soul, you must sit on this rock until you are able to explain the following lines, which are written in this sacred book: *The moon on the lake shines on the winds between the pine trees, and a long night grows quiet at midnight!*" Having said this, Ungai bowed low and left the mad priest, Joan, seated on the rock reflecting.

For a month Ungai wandered from temple to temple, lecturing. At the end of that time he came back by way of Fumonji Temple, and thought he would go up to it and see what had happened to mad Joan. At the teahouse at which he had first put up he asked the old landlady if she had seen or heard any more of the crazy priest.

"No," she said: "we have neither seen nor heard of him. Some people say he has left; but no one knows, for none dare go up to the temple to see."

"Well," said Ungai, "I will go up to-morrow morning -and find out."

Next morning Ungai went to the temple, and found Joan still seated exactly as he had left him on the rock muttering the words: "*The moon on the lake shines on the winds between the pine trees, and a long night grows quiet at midnight!*" Joan's hair and beard had become long and grey in the time, and he appeared to be miserably thin and almost transparent. Ungai was struck with pity at Joan's righteous determination and patience, and tears came to his eyes.

"Get up, get up," said he, "for indeed you are a holy and determined man."

But Joan did not move. Ungai poked him with his staff, to awaken him, as he thought; but, to his horror, Joan fell to pieces, and disappeared like a flake of melting snow.

Ungai stayed in the temple for three days, praying for the soul of Joan. The villagers, hearing of this generous action, rebuilt the temple and made him their priest. Their temple had formerly belonged to the Mitsu sect; but now it was transferred to Ungai's 'Jo do' sect, and the title or name of 'Fumonji' was changed to 'Hakkotsuzan' (White Bone Mountain). The temple is said to have prospered for hundreds of years after.

# Note

Taken from *Ancient Tales and Folklore of Japan* by Richard Gordon Smith, London, A. & C. Black [1918]. Scanned, proofed and formatted at sacred-texts.com, February 2006, by John Bruno Hare. This text is in the public domain in the United States because it was published prior to 1923.

This book is a collection of historical legends and folktales from Japan. Nearly all of them are set in a well-defined time and place, instead of 'once upon a time.' Smith does not try to dress up the language or narrative for westerners, or sentimentalize the stories. Instead, he tells each story very literally, even when they include supernatural elements. The result is an anthology of Japanese 'magical realist' tales which contemporary readers will find appealing (from www.sacred-texts.com ).

The soul, in certain spiritual, philosophical and psychological traditions, is the incorporeal essence of a person or living thing. Many philosophical and spiritual systems teach that humans are souls; some attribute souls to all living things and even to inanimate objects (such as rivers); this belief is commonly called animism, and in shamanism all life is considered to be connected in this respect too. The soul is often believed to exit the body and live on after a person's death, and some religions posit that God creates souls. The soul has often been deemed integral or essential to consciousness and personality, and is used as a synonym for spirit.

In shamanism soul loss is the term used to describe the way parts of that essence become detached when we are faced with traumatic situations. In psychological terms, it is known as dissociation and it works as a defence mechanism, a means of displacing unpleasant feelings, impulses or thoughts into the unconscious. In shamanic terms, these split off parts can be found in non-ordinary reality and are only accessible to those familiar with its topography (see Gagan, 1998, p.9). Soul retrieval entails the shaman journeying to find the missing parts and then returning them to the client seeking help. The shaman, in the words of Eliade, "is the great specialist in the human soul: he alone 'sees' it, for he knows its 'form' and its destiny" (Eliade, 1989, p.8). What we come across in this particular ballad though, can perhaps best be described as a case of soul captivation or even soul theft rather than case of soul loss.

Soul Captivation is not to be confused with Charismatic Captivation, a term used to refer to the widespread problem of authoritarian abuse in some Neo-Pentecostal church-groups that permeated the very fabric, foundation, and functions of the Neo-Pentecostal church after being introduced through a Charismatic campaign known as the Discipleship/Shepherding Movement (1970-77) [see http://www.charismatic-captivation.com]. Neither is Soul Captivation to be confused with the more commonly referred to Soul Possession, which is what we shall start by considering.

Soul Possession is a paranormal/supernatural event in which, allegedly, spirits, gods, demons, or other disincarnate or extraterrestrial entities take control of a human body, resulting in noticeable changes in the health and behaviour of the affected person. The term can also describe a similar action of taking residence in an inanimate object, such as in the case of the Golem of Prague, thereby giving it animation. Possession may be voluntary or involuntary and may be considered to have beneficial or detrimental effects.

In Haitian Vodou, for example, practitioners can be possessed by the *lwa* (or Loa). When the *lwa* descends upon a practitioner, the practitioner's body is being used by the spirit, according to the tradition. Some spirits are believed to be able to give prophecies of upcoming events or situations pertaining to the possessed one, also called *Chwal* or the 'Horse of the Spirit'. After the event, the practitioner has no recollection of the possession and not all practitioners have the ability to become possessed, but practitioners who do generally prefer not to make excessive use of it because it leaves them feeling drained.

In Christian orthodoxy, cast-down angels, or demons are disembodied angels and are able to 'demonically possess' individuals. Christians believe that there are many spirits in the world, but only the Holy Spirit is considered pure and trustworthy. They see the human body as having been created to be a temple to the living God. They also believe Jesus came to the earth to fill all things with His Holy Spirit, which is the fullness of God literally living inside of a believer.

In the Jewish tradition, possession can take the form of a *dybuk*. After three reincarnations without repair, the soul is not permitted to be reincarnated any more as a human being, and may be reincarnated only in a sub-human form. However, in very extreme cases, a soul may not even be permitted transmigration.

Prohibited from the spiritual realm, it is thrust back into the physical world with no 'body'. There, demons and spirits pursue the bodiless soul as it frantically seeks refuge from their torment. Sometimes it finds respite in a sub-human host, such as an animal, plant or inanimate object. This is different than transmigration, though, since it is not placed there with the potential for repair, rather it invades the object from without, merely seeking refuge in 'exile'.

Another possibility is that it finds 'room' in another person's body. Usually this happens when the desperate soul finds a spiritual 'breach' in a person. ... Once a soul enters such a 'breach', it cleaves tenaciously to its human host who shelters it from its pursuers. This 'cleaving', or possession, called a *dybuk,* usually takes over the person's speech and behaviour.

As for Wiccans, they believe in voluntary possession by the Goddess, connected with the sacred ceremony of Drawing down the Moon. The high priestess solicits the Goddess to possess her and speak through her.

Soul Captivation, on the other hand, (which is what Ajari Joan can be said to have fallen victim to) involves the enchantment of the affected person to such an extent that they become slaves to their emotions, and then act in what society would regard as an unbalanced manner in their relationships with those they come into contact with.

# References

Eliade, M. (1989) *Shamanism: Archaic techniques of ecstasy*, London: Arkana (first published in the USA by Pantheon Books 1964).

Gagan, J.M. (1998) *Journeying: where shamanism and psychology meet*, Santa Fe, NM: Rio Chama Publications.

# 3
# The Boy with the Magic Brush and the Golden Mountain

A folktale from China and a folktale from Russia, with the message of both being more or less the same – greed for riches brings little benefit in this life!

## The Boy with the Magic Brush

Once upon a time in a little village, a poor boy named Ma Liang was born. It was not long before his parents died, so he became an orphan. To survive he had to work for a landlord. He worked day and night.

One day, after finishing his work, he returned to his shabby bed in his shabby little house. When he passed the window of the landlord's house, he saw an artist drawing a picture for the landlord. What a beautiful scene it was! Ma Liang admired it very much. He wanted so much to have a brush to draw with.

"Would you give me a brush to draw?" he asked the landlord.

"You? Ha!" replied the landlord. "A beggar wanting to draw! Are you joking?"

At this, everyone present laughed at Ma Liang. This made him so angry that he made up his mind there and then to learn how to draw. And he vowed to draw only for the poor.

From there on, he began to practise drawing. Whatever he saw and wherever he was, he drew. Because he had no brush, he used a branch or whatever else he could get his hands on. He had no paper, so he often drew in the sand.

Years went by and Ma Liang became a good artist. Everything he drew was as lovely as if it were real. He only wished he had a brush!

One night, after practising drawing, he went to bed. Because he was so tired he began to dream very quickly. Suddenly he was in a different place. A brook led off into the distance with all kinds of flowers on both banks, and an old man stood in front of him. Ma Liang was too surprised to say a word!

"You want your own brush, don't you?" the old man asked.

"Yes, I do!" replied Ma Liang.

"Well then, I will give you a brush, but remember that you promised to draw only for the poor." With this, the old man disappeared.

"But where is the brush?" Ma Liang wondered anxiously. "Where?"

When Ma Liang awoke, he realised that it had only been a dream, but to his surprise there was a real brush in his bed. He was very pleased. The first thing he did was to draw a cock on the wall. No sooner had he finished the drawing than the cock stepped out of the wall and came to life. Ma Liang had received a magic brush!

Ma Liang began to draw for the poor. Because he could draw whatever he wanted and whatever he drew came to life, he did a lot of good with his brush. It was not long before the emperor heard the news and ordered his soldiers to bring Ma Liang to him.

The emperor met Ma Liang in his big hall. The emperor said. "I have heard that you have a magic brush that can bring whatever you draw to life. Is this true?"

"Yes," replied Ma Liang.

"Then give it to me," ordered the emperor.

"No, it's mine," responded Ma Liang.

"How dare you say that?" fumed the emperor. "I am the emperor. You must obey me!" At this, two guards snatched the brush from Ma Liang's hands.

The emperor put the brush into the hands of the most respected painter in the kingdom and asked him to draw something, but his painting did not become real. Seeing that his plan was not working, the emperor tried to persuade Ma Liang to draw something. Ma Liang, however, decided to teach the emperor a lesson.

"What would you like me to draw for you?" asked Ma Liang.

"Gold. A hill made of gold," replied the emperor.

Ma Liang began to draw, not a hill of gold, but a picture of the ocean.

"Fool, I want gold!" roared the emperor.

So Ma Liang drew an island of gold in the ocean.

"Now draw a ship," ordered the emperor. A ship soon appeared in the picture. The emperor hurriedly jumped into the ship with his guards and prime minister to set sail for the island of gold. The ship sat quietly, so the emperor once again ordered Ma Liang to draw, this time wind so that the ship could move.

Ma Liang wasted no time in drawing a violent wind that almost capsized the ship. The emperor screamed for Ma Liang to stop, but Ma Liang only drew more and more bad weather until the ship disappeared out of sight.

Ma Liang continued drawing for the poor. Both he and the poor were happy.

# The Golden Mountain

ONCE upon a time a merchant's son had too much fun spending money, and the day came when he saw himself ruined; he had nothing to eat, nothing to drink. He took a shovel and went to the market place to see if perchance somebody would hire him as a worker.

A rich, proud merchant, worth many, many thousands, came along in a gilded carriage. All the fellows at the market place, as soon as they perceived him, rushed away and hid themselves in the corners. Only one remained, and this one was our merchant's son.

"Dost thou look for work, good fellow? Let me hire thee," the very rich merchant said to him.

"So be it; that's what I came here for."

"And thy price?"

"A hundred rubles a day will be sufficient for me."

"Why so much?"

"If too much, go and look for someone else; plenty of people were around and when they saw thee coming, all of them rushed away."

"All right. To-morrow come to the landing place."

The next day, early in the morning, our merchant's son arrived at the landing; the very rich merchant was already there waiting.

They boarded a ship and went to sea. For quite a long time they journeyed, and finally they perceived an island. Upon that island there were high mountains, and near the shore something seemed to be in flames.

"Yonder is something like fire," said the merchant's son.

"No, it is my golden palace."

They landed, came ashore, and—look there! the rich merchant's wife is hastening to meet him, and along with her their young daughter, a lovely girl, prettier than you could think or even dream of.

The family met; they greeted one another and went to the palace. And along with them went their new workman. They sat around the oak table and ate and drank and were cheerful.

"One day does not count," the rich merchant said; "let us have a good time and leave work for to-morrow."

The young workman was a fine, brave fellow, handsome and stately, and the merchant's lovely daughter liked him well.

She left the room and made him a sign to follow her. Then she gave him a touchstone and a flint.

"Take it," she said; "when thou art in need, it will be useful."

The next day the very rich merchant with his hired workman went to the high golden mountain. The young fellow saw at once that there was no use trying to climb or even to crawl up.

"Well," said the merchant, "let us have a drink for courage."

And he gave the fellow some drowsy drink. The fellow drank and fell asleep.

The rich merchant took out a sharp knife, killed a wretched horse, cut it open, put the fellow inside, pushed in the shovel, and sewed the horse's skin together, and himself sat down in the bushes.

All at once crows came flying, black crows with iron beaks. They took hold of the carcass, lifted it up to the top of the high mountain, and began to pick at it.

The crows soon ate up the horse and were about to begin on

the merchant's son, when he awoke, pushed away the crows, looked around and asked out loud:

"Where am I?"

The rich merchant below answered:

"On a golden mountain; take the shovel and dig for gold."

And the young man dug and dug, and all the gold he dug he threw down, and the rich merchant loaded it upon the carts.

"Enough!" finally shouted the master. "Thanks for thy help. Farewell!"

"And I—how shall I get down?"

"As thou pleasest; there have already perished nine and ninety of such fellows as thou. With thee the count will be rounded and thou wilt be the hundredth."

The proud, rich merchant was off.

"What shall I do?" thought the poor merchant's son. "Impossible to go down! But to stay here means death, a cruel death from hunger."

And our fellow stood upon the mountain, while above the black crows were circling, the black crows with iron beaks, as if feeling already the prey.

The fellow tried to think how it all happened, and he remembered the lovely girl and what she said to him in giving him the touchstone and the flint. He remembered how she said:

"Take it. When thou art in need it will prove useful."

"I fancy she had something in mind; let us try."

The poor merchant's son took out stone and flint, struck it once and lo! Two brave fellows were standing before him.

"What is thy wish? What are thy commands?" said they.

"Take me from this mountain down to the seashore."

And at once the two took hold of him and carefully brought him down.

Our hero walks along the shore. See there! A vessel comes sailing near the island.

"Ahoy! Good people! Take me along!"

"No time to stop!" And they went sailing by. But the winds arose and the tempest was heavy.

"It seems as if this fellow over there is not an ordinary man; we had better go back and take him along," decided the sailors.

They turned the prow toward the island, landed, took the merchant's son along with them and brought him to his native town.

It was a long time, or perhaps only a short time after—who could tell?—that one day the merchant's son took again his shovel and went to the market place in search of work.

The same very rich merchant came along in his gilded carriage; and, as of old, all the fellows who saw him coming rushed away.

The merchant's son remained alone.

"Will you be my workman?"

"I will at two hundred rubles a day. If so, let us to work."

"A rather expensive fellow."

"If too expensive go to others; get a cheap man. There were plenty of people, but when thou didst appear—thou seest thyself—not one is left."

"Well, all right. Come to-morrow to the landing place."

They met at the landing place, boarded a ship and sailed toward the island.

The first day they spent rather gayly, and on the second, master and workman went to work.

When they reached the golden mountain the rich, proud merchant treated his hired man to a tumbler.

"Before all, have a drink."

"Wait, master! Thou art the head; thou must drink the first. Let me treat thee this time."

The young man had already prepared some of the drowsy stuff and he quickly mixed it with the wine and presented it to the master.

The proud merchant drank and fell sound asleep.

Our merchant's son killed a miserable old horse, cut it open, pushed his master and the shovel inside, sewed it all up and hid himself in the bushes.

All at once black crows came flying, —black crows with iron beaks; they promptly lifted up the horse with the sleeping merchant inside, bore it to the top of the mountain, and began to pick the bones of their prey.

When the merchant awoke he looked here and looked there and looked everywhere.

"Where am I?"

"Upon the golden mountain. Now if thou art strong after thy rest, do not loose time; take the shovel and dig. Dig quickly and I'll teach thee how to come down."

The proud, rich merchant had to obey and dug and dug. Twelve big carts were loaded.

"Enough!" shouted the merchant's son. "Thank thee, and farewell!"

"And I?"

"And thou mayst do as thou wishest! There are already ninety and nine fellows perished before thee; with thyself there will be a hundred."

The merchant's son took along with him the twelve heavy carts with gold, arrived at the golden palace and married the lovely girl; the rich merchant's daughter became mistress of all her father's wealth, and the merchant's son with his family moved to a large town to live.

And the rich merchant, the proud, rich merchant?

He himself, like his many victims, became the prey of the black crows, black crows with iron beaks.

Well, sometimes it happens just so.

*Folk Tales from the Russian* retold by Verra Xenophontovna Kalamatiano de Blumenthal [1903] Scanned, proofed and formatted at sacred-texts.com by John Bruno Hare, March 2002. This text is in the public domain in the US because it was published prior to 1923.

# 4
# The Legend of Amirani

Amirani (Georgian: ამირანი) is the name of a Georgian hero-figure who resembles the Classical Prometheus, son of the Goddess Dali and renowned as a hunter.

Georgian myths describe how Amirani fights Devi (ogres), challenges the Gods, kidnaps Kamar (the daughter of Gods)*, and teaches metallurgy to humans. In punishment, the Gods chain Amirani to a cliff in the Caucasus Mountains, where the Titan continues to defy the Gods and struggles to break the chains; an eagle ravages his liver every day, but it heals at night. Amirani's loyal dog, in the meantime, licks the chain to thin it out, but every year, on Thursday or in some versions the day before Christmas, the Gods send smiths to repair it. In some versions, every seven years the cave where Amirani is chained can be seen in the Caucasus.

Scholars agree that this folk epic about Amirani must have been formed in the third millennium BCE and later went through numerous transformations, the most important of them being the fusion of pagan and Christian elements after the spread of Christianity. It is possible that the myth could have been assimilated by the Greek colonists or travellers and then embodied in the corpus of the famous

---

\* Kamar was believed to be the daughter of the god of nature and sky. She was famous for her beauty, which enchanted Amirani, resulting in him to kidnapping her from her heavenly abode.

Greek myth of Prometheus. In Georgian literature and culture, Amirani is often used as a symbol of the Georgian nation, its ordeals and struggle for survival, which is why it was decided to present an extended version of the legend in this volume.

There was, there was, and yet there was not. There was a hunter by the name of Sulukmakhi and he had two sons: Badri and Usup. Sulukmakhi was an experienced and well-known hunter. One day, as usual, he went hunting but could not get back home in time. It was getting dark and he had to find a place to stay overnight. He came upon a cave under a cliff. The Goddess Dali lived on that cliff. At midnight he heard the terrifying cries of a woman, and he jumped up to find out what was going on. He walked all around the cliff, but could not find any stairs to climb up. In the morning, he went to the village and asked a stonecutter to make some steps for him. The stonecutter obliged so that Sulukmakhi could scale the cliff, and when he reached the top, he found a woman lying there.

"Why are you crying so?" He asked her.

"I'm the famous Goddess Dali. One night, when I was asleep, a hunter by the name of Tsamtsumi sneaked into my bed, and because he was holding me by my golden plaits I couldn't get away from him. Now the time of my death has come. So take this knife, cut my stomach open – there is a live child there – and take him. For it would be a crime for me to take a live child to the grave with me. If this child had a chance to stay in my womb as long as normal children do, he or she would have been a great hero. As for the child, if it's a boy you must call him Amirani but, if it's a girl, you can call her whatever you like. You have to keep the child in the body of a pregnant dead cow for three days and nights and one day and night in the corpse of a buffalo. That way the child will be able to grow." – So said Dali.

Sulukmakhi cut Dali open straight away and took a beautiful boy from her womb. He called the child Amirani as Dali had told him to. Then he took the child home, kept him for three days and nights in the corpse of a cow and one day and night in a buffalo, just as he had been instructed to do. After that, he brought him up with his other two sons. The brothers and the mother loved little Amirani dearly. Sulukmakhi was a poor man, and his wish was to somehow find a rich godfather for his child. His wish was granted, for at the boy's christening, God came and said to Sulukmakhi, "I would like to christen him."

Sulukmakhi couldn't say no to God. So God christened him and blessed him to be as quick as the rough river Mtkvari, to have knees as strong as a wolf, and to have the strength of an ox. And this is how Amirani grew up to be as strong as he did.

Before his death, Sulukmakhi said to his sons: "When I die, I have to warn you that some devi will start fighting with you. You have to leave this place and move to another." Then he gave them the directions of the place they were to move to. Soon after that, Sulukmakhi passed away and the children became orphans.

We, Badri, Usup and Amirani

Became orphans

Frightened by Devis

Moved to Chabalkhi

When Amirani grew up, this is what he said to his brothers: "We need to go and do something or else we'll starve to death here." And the brothers agreed that it was the only sensible thing to do.

> Three brothers Badri, Usup and Amirani
>
> Crossed the nine mountains
>
> Came to the tenth- Mount Algeti.
>
> They saw a castle there
>
> Built out of crystal, it was.
>
> For nine days and nights
>
> They went round and round it in circles
>
> But couldn't find the door.
>
> So Amirani kicked at the castle wall
>
> And that became the door.
>
> Behind the door
>
> They found a body
>
> Pitiful and poor,
>
> In his hand a book
>
> And this is what was written in it:
>
> "If you can kill Devi-Baq'baq,
>
> You can have my rashi;*

---

\* A rashi is a magical winged horse. Rashi can be of different kinds. Those of land were well disposed to humans and heroes and could foretell the future. Rashi of the seas were more hostile to humans but could take heroes to the depth of the sea while their milk was believed to cure many illnesses. Heavenly rashi were winged and fire-breathing animals, very difficult to subdue but then forever loyal to their riders.

If you can kill Devi-Baq'baq,

You can have my castle;

If you can kill Devi-Baq'baq,

You can have my wife and all my gold;

And if you ask who I am

I can tell you

I'm the nephew of Usup."

"Let's go and kill Baq'baq' Devi, and then we can have all his wealth," Amirani said to his brothers.

Usup refused, though. "We'll be accused of robbing the dead if we do that," he said.

Anyway, Amirani and his brothers left, and on the way they met Baq'baq' Devi.

"Where are you going?" The brothers asked him.

"I was told the hunter Tsumtsumi has passed away and so I'm going to eat him."

"Go back home at once. Nobody will let you eat human flesh," Amirani said to him. But he refused to, so Amirani and Baq'baq' Devi started to fight:

Amirani and Devi are fighting

The fields are trembling

Amirani throws Devi down

Makes him cry out in pain

Because he falls down

On a rock

And breaks his shoulder.

Then this was what the devi said:

"Wait, wait, Amirani don't kill me

And I'll tell you about the most beautiful woman

She lives on the other side of the river

Her name is Kamar

Go and fight for her

If you really want a fight.

I'll send my guide to you

Who will show you

How to get to her."

The devi had ten heads and Amirani cut off nine of them.
"Can you leave me with my last head on?" The devi asked.
"No, I have to cut that off too." Amirani replied.
"Then I have one last request,'" continued the devi. "From my last head three worms will appear. Let them go free at least."
Amirani cut off his tenth head and let the worms go free, as the devi had requested him to do.
Then his brother Usup said to him: "Kill the worms too. You got rid of one problem, now get rid of the second one.'"
"The first evil could not harm me, so I don't suppose the second one can either!' Amirani responded.
The worms turned into dragons, though, and when he brothers continued on their way, they were confronted by these dragons.
"Don't say I didn't warn you. You can go and fight with them on your own now!" Usup said to his brother.
Amirani killed one dragon, then the second one, but the third

one swallowed him. Usup got angry and shot an arrow at him, so removing a metre off the dragon's tail. The dragon left to digest Amirani, but his tail couldn't reach his mouth any more so it was difficult for him.

"I've got a stomach ache." The dragon complained to its mother.

"Did you swallow Darejan's son then?" His mother replied. "If you did, that would explain things. You'll find digesting him is impossible!"

Meanwhile, Amirani has a knife in his pocket. He cuts through the dragon from inside, and manages to get out that way. Then he killed the dragon's mother too. His brothers Badri and Usup now join him. They have a meal together, a little rest, and then continue on their way in search of Kamar.

Baq'baq' davi's guide, though, was intentionally making their journey more complicated then necessary. Usup realised this and at the crossroads, he marked a log with his arrow. On the third day, they came to the same place again and Usup found his arrow. He said to Amirani:

Amiran, can't you see

What he's doing to us?

This is the third time

We've come back to the same place –

The place where I left my arrow

So Amirani killed the guide. and then they came to a castle. A lot of noise was coming from inside. Amirani called out to the host to open the gates.

The castle belonged to the devi, who sent their sister to see who was there.

"Go out and see who calls us," they said to her. "We need to be careful though, in case those people are Darejan's sons. You'll be able to recognize Amirani easily because he has huge eyes and a golden tooth."

The woman goes out to try to find out who they are. She is smiling at Amirani, and this is what he says to her:

"Why are you smiling at me, devi woman,

Why are you showing me your white teeth?

You're walking up and down

To check my face and teeth, aren't you!"

When the woman saw his golden tooth, she ran into the castle to warn her brothers. But Amirani follows after her and fights with the devi, killing all of them. The door is locked though, and the room fills up with blood. Amirani is drowning. So he picks up one of the devi and throws him against the door. The door bursts open and the blood flows away. Amirani is saved.

The brothers came to a river. Amirani knew Usup had a great Tetrovana [the name for a white horse] so he asked if he could borrow it. At first Usup did not want to give it to him because he said he was tired of looking for Kamar, but in the end he agreed. Amirani sat on the horse and crossed the river on it. Kamar is sitting in the castle. Amirani goes up to her and says: "You're are coming with me because I am marrying you." Kamar was a daughter of the king of the elephants. Her father had the legs of a human but the body of an elephant. Kamari was doing the washing up while she spoke to Amirani.

"Put the dishes away, but be careful not to break anything or else my father will be told." Amirani dropped one plate three times, though, which made him angry, so he took the plate and threw it on the floor. One of the broken pieces spoke to another broken bit, the whole to the whole, and word of what had happened reached the king that way. Meanwhile, Amirani left the castle, taking Kamar away with him. Kamar took a pinch of salt, a comb and a mirror with her, and the Elephant King gathered his army to follow them both.

While Amirani and Kamar were crossing the river, a strong gale started to blow. Kamar knew that it was her father who was causing this. 'It's my my father, he is following us," she said. She then took the comb and threw it behind her, making a thick forest appear. But the king managed to cross the forest, and the strong gale started to blow again. This time Kamar threw a pinch of salt behind her, making a bare cliff appear. The king managed to cross this too, though, and then the wind started up once again. This time Kamar threw the mirror, making an enormous sea appear. But this did not work either, as most of the king's soldiers managed to cross this too. So Amirani and Kamar went back to the castle they had come from and very soon the King's army followed them there.

"Come on Usup. Surely you have to fight with them now," said Amirani. And Usup agreed.

"But don't you start fighting until my sword stops shining, and as long as it shines then don't," Usup said.

Usup fought bravely for a long time, but when the brothers saw that his sword was not shining any more, then Badri joined the fight. He said the same thing to Amirani that Usup had said to him, and Badri fought ferociously for a long time too. When Kamar saw that

Badri has also been killed, she woke up Amirani, and this time he went to fight with the army.

Now the King of the Elephants had a lathe which he was turning himself and more and, as he did so, more and more new solders appeared. Amirani fought until he got to the lathe, then struck it with his sword and broke it. That stopped the soldiers from multiplying, and so he managed to kill them all off. Finally Amirani and the Elephant King started to fight. With the king having the hide of an elephant instead of skin, Amirani's sword could do nothing. Kamar saw this and shouted down to Amirani from the castle wall from where she was watching the battle take place:

"Come on Amirani,

Everyone admires your bravery

And can see you can fight really well,

But use your brain too.

Don't strike the elephant on its back,

But strike him down below."

Amirani heard what she was saying, and with just one blow of his mighty sword, sliced off both the king's legs.

"Look at that cruel Kamar," the king cried out in pain,

"And look at who she chooses over her father!

If I get to you,

I'll slit your throat."

But Amirani cut up the king of the elephants and went to join Kamar. But she told him that there was still work to do, and sent him off to find his brothers.

So Amirani looked for his brothers among the dead solders on the battlefield, found them both, and placed their bodies together, side by side. "Now I have to die with my brothers" he says. He tries to kill himself with his own sword but try as he might, he just cannot do it. At that point a kaji appears, and this is what he says to him

"If you want to die, you need to cut your little finger with your sword and let the blood flow out. And that's the only way to do it."

So Amirani cut his finger, the blood poured out, and it worked just as the kaji told him it would. On seeing the man she loved die before her own very eyes, Kamar broke down and wept uncontrollably. Then a little mouse crept out of its hole, and started to drink the blood of the dead. Kamar struck the mouse with a whip and killed it, though. At that point a second mouse appeared on the scene, and this is what he said to her:

"Hey, you cruel woman, because of you so many people have died, and even your husband and your brothers-in-law are now lying dead in front of you. And although I'm only small and seemingly insignificant, I can bring the mouse you killed back to life easily, without any problem. Just watch me."

And this is what he did. The mouse found a three-leafed clover, picked it, rubbed it over the mouse that Kamar had killed, and brought it back to life again. So Kamar, on seeing that, did the same with Amirani, and brought him and his brothers back to life this way.

They all left for the castle together. After that, Amirani showed even more bravery. He killed loads of Devi and other evil spirits too, and there nobody who could defeat him.

One day Amirani met the sister of a famous hero called Ambri. She was carrying her dead brother, and taking him to be buried. One of Ambri's legs was sticking out and and dragging along the ground.

"Lift his leg for me please, and place it back on the cart," Ambri's sister asked Amirani.

Amirani tried to lift the leg but he was not able to. Then the sister tried, and she did it by herself in the end. And this is what she said to him:

God knows Amirani,

That you cannot compare to Ambri

When he was alive he was better than you,

And dead he still is.

Nobody could defeat Amirani on this earth, though. He killed all the devi so there was not one single one left. One day he was walking on Mount Ialbuz [Elbrus] and met his godfather, God, on the way. And this is what Amirani said to him:

"Why did you give me such power so that there is nobody in this world who can defeat me? So come on, you fight with me now!"

God is an old man with a stick in his hand

"I will hummer my stick in the ground and let's see if you can get it out," God said. He hammered the stick into the ground and Amirani pulled it out without any problem. For a second time God hammered in the stick, and Amirani pulled it out again.

"Why you are playing games with me?" Amirani asked God. Then God said a prayer and made the stick grow roots into the earth. Now Amirani tries to pull it out but he cannot. Then God threw a chain over this stick and chained Amirani to it. Every day he is allowed one loaf a bread and a glass of water, and he is guarded by q'ursha [a dog's name].

The dog licks at the chain constantly, day after day, year after year. Amirani has a hammer in his hand. Every Good Friday, a wagtail flies to the top of the mountain and sits on the chain. Amirani tries to hit it with the hammer, but the wagtail flies away and the stick is driven even deeper into the ground.

Q'ursha keeps licking at the chain, and when the chain is nearly ready to break, on "Red Thursday" [the day before Good Friday], all the blacksmiths strike their anvils with their hammers and then the chain becomes whole again. Ever since that time, Amirani has remained chained to Mount Ialbuzi. And if he should succeed in breaking the chain, for sure he will destroy everything, and first on his list will be all the blacksmiths.

\* \* \*

Georgian paganism is perhaps best described as a revealed religion, not one that was revealed at the beginning of historical time by means of speech that has been preserved orally or in writing, as is the case with Judaism or Islam, but one that is made manifest each time the soul of a human being is possessed by a Hat´i (a divinity). That person, who is then regarded as being officially possessed, becomes a sort of shaman and is known as a Kadag. "When the Kadag goes into trance, on the occasion of a religious ritual or an event marking individual or collective life, he speaks, and it is then the god who is speaking through his mouth" (Bonnefoy, 1993, p.255). The priest-sacrificer is similarly chosen by what can be termed divine election made manifest through possession. His function however is multi-purpose, not only to perform rites but also to act as the political and military chief of the community.

"Horizontal" inspirational practices – those which are available, in principle, to any member of the society, and which are marked by trance and possession – became marginalised in this way over time, in favour of the institution of "vertical" inspiration, which is based on esoteric knowledge controlled by priest-like specialists, a phenomenon which often accompanies increasing sociopolitical complexification and centralization (see Hugh-Jones 1996).

A shamanic initiation is one in which the shaman symbolically dies and is reborn, and the healing of the protagonist in many legends and folktales parallels what takes place in shamanic initiation rites. The legend of Amirani, who is brought back to life with the help of a mouse that can be regarded as a spirit helper, provides just one of numerous examples.

> In the archaic mythological mindset illness was the loss of the wholeness of the body whereas healing was seen as the regaining of wholeness [much the same way as many practitioners of alternative medicine see illness today]. In a series of Armenian folktales [and this can be applied to legends and folktales in general] the hero is killed, dissected, and then parts of his body are collected by some magic helpers and put together after which he comes back to life (often with the help of apples of life or water of life). In fact, illness is seen as an equivalent to death, and recovery is regarded as resurrection (Zaqarian, 2009, p.66).

# References

Berman, M., Kalandadze, K., Kuparidze, G., & Rusieshvili, M. (2011) *Georgia through its Folklore, Legends, and People*, New York: Nova Publishers Inc.

Bonnefoy, Y. (comp.) (1993) *American, African and Old European Mythologies*, Chicago and London, The University of Chicago Press.

Hugh-Jones, Stephen. (1996) 'Shamans, prophets, priest and pastors' In N. Thomas & C. Humphrey, eds. *Shamanism, history and the state*, Ann Arbor: U Mich Press, pp 32-75.

Zaqarian, Yeva. (2009) 'A Mode of Ritual Healing' in *Voske Divan: Journal of fairy-tale studies*, 2009 vol. 1, Yerevan: Hovhannes Toumanian Museum.

# 5
# The Story of Jumping Mouse

This version of a Plains Indian Sundance story was told to Robin Ridington by his friend and teacher, Chuck Storm, Hyemeyohsts. Robin Ridington told the story, with notes, to the Annual Meeting of the American Anthropological Society in New Orleans, Nov. 22, 1969.

The story is about a seemingly simple mouse, who dares to question what is out of the ordinary and seek out the truth. He shows curiosity, which leads him to new ideas. When he has his experience at the river, he is given a new name, which signifies his own personal growth. However, when he takes his newfound ideas back to his people, they don't believe him because they are far too different than what they already know, and they decide for this reason that he is harmful. Their attitude reflects society in general – in how so many of the decisions people make are based on fear of the unknown, fear that comfort felt in one's present situation will be lost in the new situation. And this results in their wish to stick to what they are familiar with and to resist all forms of change.

Facing the unknown requires courage, but the fact remains that it is only in regions of danger that one can find "the treasure hard to attain" (Jung in *Psychology and Alchemy*). And our job as the relatives, friend or educators of those we love or are responsible for caring for, is to provide the right conditions for them to undertake such journeys, to empower them so they have the confidence to explore such regions, initially together with us, but then on their own.

* * *

One time there was a mouse who lived with other mice and this little mouse kept hearing a roaring in his ears. He couldn't figure out what it was. All the time, everywhere he went, as he went about his mouse's business, his little whiskers going, looking into nooks and crannies, gathering things, taking seeds from one place to another, he kept hearing this roaring and he wondered what it was. Sometimes he would ask the other mice, "I hear this roaring in my ears, what is it?" And the other mice always said, "We don't hear anything. You must be crazy, get back to work. Accumulate!" So he got back to work, being a mouse, and did all the things that mice do, but he couldn't get the roaring out of his ears and finally he resolved that he would try to find out what it was.

Very timidly he went just to the edge of where the mice were living around the roots of trees and bushes. As soon as he got outside of where the mice lived, he saw a raccoon and the racoon said, "Hello, little brother," and he looked up and said, "Hello, brother." And he said, "You know, I hear this roaring in my ears all the time and I wonder what it is." The raccoon said, "Oh, that's easy. I know what that is, that's the great river and I go there every day to wash my food." Little Mouse was really excited because this was the first time that anyone had ever said that what he heard was real and so he started scheming in his mouse's way about how he would take the proof back to all the other mice and then they wouldn't think he was strange anymore. So racoon said, "Yes, I'll take you to the river," and little mouse followed along behind him.

Finally they got to the edge of the great river, to a little eddy on the great river, but little mouse had never seen anything like that before in his life, this fantastic expanse of water. Where mice live the only water they see is rainwater and dew. They don't see big bodies of water, and to little mouse it was just immense and he timidly went up to the edge of the water. He looked in and he freaked because he saw a mouse in there! He jumped back but nothing happened and he looked again and he saw, yes, it's a mouse in there. He'd seen his own reflection for the first time.

The raccoon led him down to the bank of the river and at one place he put his hand in and tasted the water and finally the racoon said, "I have to go about my business and find food and wash it in the river, but I'll take you to a friend of mine." So raccoon took little mouse to his brother, Frog.

There was a big green frog sitting on the edge of the river, sort of half in and half out. Little mouse said to him, "Hello, brother," and the frog replied, "Hello, brother." And they talked for awhile and the frog told him all about his life, about how he had been given the gift to live half in the water and half out of the water. He was all green on top and white underneath. He told little mouse, "When thunderbird flies you will always find me here but when winter- man comes I will be gone." That sounded pretty good to little mouse and then the frog said to him, "Do you want a medicine?" Little mouse said, "Sure, I'd like a medicine, yes." And then the frog said, "O. K., just crouch down as low as you can get and then jump up as high as you can jump."

So little mouse did that. He got down as low as he could go and then he jumped up as high as a mouse could jump. And when he jumped up he saw the sacred mountains and then he fell back down and fell into the water.

Nothing like this had ever happened to him before and he scurried out of the water and he was really mad. He said, "You tricked me, that's no medicine, I fell in the water." And the frog said, "Yes, you fell in the water. You're wet. But you're safe, you're alive, aren't you?" And little mouse said, "Yes, I am." And the frog said to him, "What did you see when you jumped up?" Little mouse said, "Oh, yes, yes. I saw the sacred mountains." And the frog said to him, "You have a new name. Your name is Jumping Mouse."

Jumping Mouse thanks the frog for having taught him and then he says, "It's time to go back to my people. I want to tell them about the sacred mountains." He has really changed. Instead of saying, "I want to prove to those bastards that the river really exists," now he is just excited. He's seen the sacred mountains and he wants to go back and share his vision with his people. He speaks in innocence because he has learned from the frog. He wants to go back in innocence to tell them about it, and in innocence he will be able to return. The frog tells him, "It's easy to go back to your people. Just keep the sound of the river behind you. The roaring that you heard is now your medicine. You know what it is and you can return to your people."

Mice are unable to go in a straight line because they can see close but with the medicine behind him Jumping Mouse can return. He has always heard it, but now he can navigate by it, he has a direction.

Jumping Mouse keeps the medicine behind him and goes back to where the other mice are living. He says to them, "You know that roaring in my ears? It was the great river and racoon took me there and I met a frog. The frog gave me a medicine and I jumped up and I saw the sacred mountains." But they looked at him really strangely because he was all wet. He had forgotten entirely about falling in the river but they started whispering among themselves. They said, "An animal must have had him in its mouth. There must be something wrong with him. There must be some pollution, something terrible that he was in the jaws of death and wasn't taken. Very dangerous person." They didn't even hear what he said about the sacred mountains.

Poor Jumping Mouse was just crestfallen at this because he had really wanted to tell them about what he had seen so they could see it too, but they couldn't. You cannot see through the eyes of another without giving him your eyes, and they were unable to do that. He stayed with them for a while because they were his people, but finally he resolved that he would go on and find the sacred mountains.

He told them about his resolve and they said, "You're insane, you can't do it, the spots will get you." They knew, all mice know, that out on the prairie eagles can swoop down and get mice. But mice do not know eagles. They are too distant from them and so they only see them as spots in the sky. They can see close into the little things of the earth but when they look up and far away they only see spots. And this is a paradox, but eagles when they are close to the ground only see things as a blur. The mice's fear of spots is real because eagles are real and really get mice, and Jumping Mouse was terrified but went on. Out onto the prairie he went, his whiskers feeling, dodging this way and that, feeling the spots pressing down on his back. The prairie is where the great animals meet and travel far and it is an alien place for a mouse. Jumping Mouse went out into it with his fear and finally he came to a circle of sweet sage.

The circle of sage was a haven, a cover from the spots, and sweet sage is a plant that you cannot eat but which is used by the Indians for incense, prayer, something healing and beautiful. There in the sweet sage was an old, old mouse. Long braids, an old mouse. Jumping Mouse was joyous to meet someone of his own kind he could talk to out in this alien place. The clump of sage was a haven and a paradise for mice. There were seeds and roots to crawl into and everything a mouse could want there. He went up to the old mouse and he said, "Grandfather, I heard a roaring in my ears and I have been to the great river." The old mouse said, "Yes, I too heard the roaring and I too have been to the great river." Jumping Mouse was really excited because for the first time he had found a mouse who had shared his experience. So they talked about the river and the common things they knew. Jumping Mouse was more and more excited and he said, "And then I met the frog and he told me to jump up and I jumped up and I saw the sacred mountains." The old mouse was silent for a long time and finally said, "My grandson, the great river is real and we have both been there and tasted its water, but the sacred mountains are just a myth. They don't exist." Jumping Mouse was just crushed and disappointed by this and the old mouse said to him, "Stay with me and grow old with me here. This is a perfect place for mice and we have both been further than any other mouse."

Jumping Mouse resolves to go on and the old mouse is really upset. He says, "You can't do that, the spots will get you." But Jumping Mouse is resolved and he leaves the old mouse in the sage. He goes out onto the prairie and he is really afraid. He can feel the spots, just feel them pressing in. Knows that they are there every moment; his little whiskers are going fast and finally he gets out to the middle of the prairie and comes to a stand of chokecherry bushes. Chokecherries are good to eat but they make you fantastically thirsty. The more you eat, the more thirst you have.

Jumping Mouse is out of breath and thankful for a safe haven and cover from the spots and as he lies there panting, he hears a great sighing slowly, up and down. And he looks up and sees that it is a great animal. Jumping Mouse thinks, "I am so small and this great being is so large," and he forgets his fear in his awe and goes up to the animal and says, "Hello, great brother," and it replies, "Hello, little brother," and Jumping Mouse asks, "Who are you?" and he says, "I am a buffalo and I am dying." When he hears this, little mouse is overcome with sadness that this great being that he has just met is dying and he says to him, "What can I do to make you well? Is there any medicine that will make you well?" And the buffalo says, "I have talked with my medicine and it has told me that there is only one thing that will make me well, and that is the eye of a mouse, and there is no such thing as a mouse."

Jumping Mouse was just freaked by this and he ran back, his little whiskers going, his tail behind him until he reached some cover. But from a safe place he heard the breathing again, getting slower and slower, and he felt a tremendous compassion for the buffalo. "I am so small," he thought, "and the buffalo is so great and so beautiful." Finally he came out from his hole, taking two steps forward and one step back, his tail dragging, but resolved to speak to his great brother. "I want to tell you something," he said, " there is such a thing as a mouse and I am a mouse."

"Thank you very much, little brother," the buffalo replied. "I will die happy knowing that there is such a thing as a mouse. But it is too much to ask of you to give one of your eyes." But Jumping Mouse told him, "No, I am so small and you are so great that I would like to give you one of my eyes and make you well." And immediately as he said that, one of his eyes flew out of his head and the buffalo jumped up, strong and powerful, his hooves pounding on the earth and his great head dancing and hooking. He was strong and he said, "I know who you are. You are Jumping Mouse and you have been to the river and jumped up and seen the sacred mountains. You are on your way to them. I can guide you across the prairie, for I am one of the great beings of the prairie. Run underneath me. I know you are afraid of the spots, and I will protect you from them. You will be safe and I will take you across the prairie right to the edge of the sacred mountains. But I can't take you farther than that because I am a creature of the prairie and I must stay here to give away to the people. If I go up onto the sacred mountains it will be too steep and I will fall and crush you."

So Jumping Mouse runs underneath the buffalo across the prairie, his hooves just pounding, dust flying, shaking the earth and little mouse is frightened at the great power of the buffalo. He knows he is safe but this is worse, trying to keep up with a goddam buffalo! Finally they get to the edge of the prairie and he is really exhausted and he comes creeping out from underneath the great buffalo, thankful to be alive. He looks up at the great gift and he says, "That was really something!" And the buffalo says, "You didn't need to worry, little brother. I am a buffalo and I know where I place every footstep. I am a great dancer and light on my feet. I could see you underneath me all the way and you were perfectly safe."

So the buffalo left Jumping Mouse at the edge of the sacred mountains, and he looks around. Who should he see now but a wolf, sitting there - a big beautiful wolf, just sitting on his haunches, kind of looking around one place or another. And he goes up to him and he says, "Hello, brother Wolf." And the wolf says, "Wolf, wolf, yes, I'm a wolf, wolf, yes, wolf," and then he sort of sits back and a beatific grin comes across his and he doesn't say any more. His mind wanders, slips away. And Jumping Mouse can't figure that out. What the hell's going on? So he comes up again and he says, "Hello, brother wolf," and the wolf says "Wolf, wolf, yes wolf, wolf yes, I'm a wolf, yes," and his voice trails off as his mind slips again.

So Jumping Mouse wonders what is going on and he goes a little distance away and he listens to the beating of his heart; the sound of his heart is beating like a drum inside him. And he remembered all the things that have happened to him. He remembered that when the buffalo was dying the thing that would make him well was the eye of a mouse and he figures that's good medicine. "I've got good medicine, a lot of power in the eye of a mouse." And he resolves that he will give his other eye to the wolf and that will make him well. So he goes up to the wolf and he says, "Brother wolf," and the wolf begins to say, "Wolf, wolf" but Jumping Mouse stops him and says, "I want to give you one of my eyes," and immediately his eye, his last eye, is gone and he's blind, and the wolf jumps up and says, "Yes, I'm a wolf. I know who you are. You are Jumping Mouse. You have been to the great river, the frog has shown you the sacred mountains, the buffalo has brought you to me, and I can guide you to the medicine lake at the top of the sacred mountains."

Little mouse is blind now, and all he has is his whiskers. He can touch but he has given up all his old ways of seeing. He can only touch things close now. The wolf takes him up from the prairie, through the pines, 'stands-in-place.' Finally they get to the open country at the top of the mountain. There are no trees there, no cover, nothing for a mouse. They get to the edge of the medicine lake and the wolf tells him, "We are here. We are at the medicine lake." And he sits Jumping Mouse down by it.

Jumping Mouse takes his hand and puts it in the water and tastes it, and it's good, it's beautiful. And then the wolf describes to him what he can see in the medicine lake. He says, "In the medicine lake are reflected all the lodges of the people. The whole world is reflected there. The medicine lake is the reflection. It is a symbol of the reflection. They sit there and Jumping Mouse knows that it is time for the wolf to go about his business and travel to other parts of the world. It is time for the eagles to get him. It is an open place and as soon as his guide is gone the eagles will see him and come. He is blind and he can't see them. The wolf feels tremendous compassion and feeling for Jumping Mouse his brother, and his heart stretches out to him, and the wolf cries. Then he leaves and Jumping Mouse is left alone, blind, nothing but looking within, and he can feel the spots on his back, just pressing in, hard. And then he hears the rush of wind and wings and then there is a fantastic shock and everything is black.

The next thing he knows, he can see colours. He can see! He can see colours. And he's amazed, astounded, he doesn't know if he's dreaming or what is happening. But he's alive and he can see colours. Then he sees a blur of colours moving toward him, something green and white moving his way and from the colours comes a voice. "You want a medicine?" And Jumping Mouse says, "Yes, I'd like a medicine." And the voice says, "Just get down as far as you can and jump up as high as you can jump." So little mouse gets down as low as he can and jumps up as high as he can jump, and when he does, the wind catches him and swirls him up and up and up in the air. And the voice calls out from below him, "Grab hold of the wind!" So little mouse reaches out and grabs hold of the wind as hard as he can, and the wind takes him higher and higher until everything begins to get clearer and clearer. Crystal clear, and he can see all the great beings of the prairie, the buffalo, the wolf on the mountain, and he looks down into the medicine lake and there are all the lodges of the people reflected, and on the edge of the medicine lake he sees his friend the frog. He calls down to him, "Hello, brother Frog," and the frog calls back to him, "Hello, brother Eagle."

# The Story of Jumping Mouse version (2) This version, is from *Seven Arrows,* by Hyemeyohsts Storm

### Once there was a Mouse.

He was Busy Mouse, Searching Everywhere, Touching his Whiskers to the Grass, and Looking. He was Busy as all Mice are, Busy with Mice things. But Once in a while he would Hear an Odd Sound. He would Lift his Head, Squinting hard to See, his Whiskers Wiggling in the air, and he would Wonder.

One Day he Scurried up to a fellow Mouse and asked him, "Do you Hear a Roaring in your Ears, my Brother?"

"No, no," answered the Other Mouse, not Lifting his Busy Nose from the Ground. "I Hear Nothing. I am Busy now. Talk to me Later."

He asked Another Mouse the same Question and the Mouse Looked at him Strangely.

"Are you Foolish in your Head? What Sound?" he asked and Slipped into a Hole in a Fallen Cottonwood Tree.

The little Mouse shrugged his Whiskers and Busied himself again, Determined to Forget the Whole Matter. But there was that Roaring again. It was faint, very faint, but it was there! One Day, he decided to investigate the Sound just a little. Leaving the Other Busy Mice, he Scurried a little Way away and Listened again. There It was! He was Listening hard when suddenly, Someone said Hello.

"Hello, little Brother," the Voice said, and Mouse almost Jumped right Out of his Skin. He Arched his Back and Tail and was about to Run.

"Hello," again said the Voice. "It is I, Brother Raccoon." And sure enough, It was!

"What are you Doing Here all by yourself, little Brother?" asked the Raccoon. The Mouse blushed, and put his Nose almost to the Ground. "I Hear a Roaring in my Ears and I am Investigating it," he answered timidly.

"A Roaring in your Ears?" replied the Raccoon as he Sat Down with him. "What you Hear, little Brother, is the River."

"The River?" Mouse asked curiously. "What is a River?"

"Walk with me and I will Show you the River," Raccoon said.

Little Mouse was terribly Afraid, but he was Determined to Find Out Once and for All about the Roaring.

"I can Return to my Work," he thought, "after this thing is Settled, and possibly this thing may Aid me in All my Busy Examining and Collecting. And my Brothers All said it was Nothing. I will Show them. I will Ask Raccoon to Return with me and I will have Proof."

"All right Raccoon, my Brother," said Mouse. "Lead on to the River. I will Walk with you."

Little Mouse Walked with Raccoon. His little Heart was Pounding in his Breast. The Raccoon was Taking him upon Strange Paths and little Mouse Smelled the scent of many things that had Gone by this Way. Many times he became so Frightened he almost Turned Back. Finally, they Came to the River! It was Huge and Breathtaking, Deep and Clear in Places, and Murky in Others. Little Mouse was unable to See Across it because it was so Great. It Roared, Sang, Cried, and Thundered on its Course. Little Mouse Saw Great and Little Pieces of the World Carried Along on its Surface.

"It is Powerful!" little Mouse said, Fumbling for Words.

"It is a Great thing," answered the Raccoon, "but here, let me Introduce you to a Friend."

In a Smoother, Shallower Place was a Lily Pad, Bright and Green. Sitting upon it was a Frog, almost as Green as the Pad it sat on. The

Frog's White Belly stood out Clearly.

"Hello, little Brother," said the Frog. "Welcome to the River."

"I must Leave you Now," cut in Raccoon, "but do not Fear, little Brother, for Frog will Care for you Now." And the Raccoon Left, Looking along the River Bank for Food that he might Wash and Eat.

Little Mouse Approached the Water and Looked into it. He saw a Frightened Mouse Reflected there.

"Who are you?" little Mouse asked the Reflection. "Are you not Afraid, being that Far out into the Great River?"

"No," answered the Frog, "I am not Afraid. I have been Given the Gift from Birth to Live both Above and Within the River. When Winter Man Comes and Freezes this Medicine, I cannot be Seen. But all the while Thunderbird Flies, I am here. To Visit me, One must Come when the World is Green. I, my Brother, am the Keeper of the Water."

"Amazing!" little Mouse said at last, again Fumbling for Words.

"Would you like to have some Medicine Power?" Frog asked.

"Medicine Power? Me?" asked little Mouse. "Yes, yes! If it is Possible."

"Then Crouch as Low as you Can, and then Jump as High as you are Able! You will have your Medicine!" Frog said.

Little Mouse did as he was Instructed. He Crouched as Low as he Could and Jumped. And when he did, his Eyes Saw the Sacred Mountains.

Little Mouse could hardly Believe his Eyes. But there They were! But then he Fell back to Earth, and he Landed in the River!

Little Mouse became Frightened and Scrambled back to the Bank. He was Wet, and Frightened nearly to Death.

"You have Tricked me," little Mouse Screamed at the Frog.

"Wait," said the Frog. "You are not Harmed. Do not let your Fear and Anger Blind you. What did you See?"

"I," Mouse stammered, "I, I Saw the Sacred Mountains!"

"And you have a New Name!" Frog said. "It is Jumping Mouse."

"Thank you. Thank you," Jumping Mouse said, and Thanked him again. "I want to Return to my People and Tell them of this thing that has Happened to me."

"Go. Go then," Frog said. "Return to your People. It is Easy to Find them. Keep the Sound of the Medicine River to the Back of your Head. Go Opposite to the Sound and you will Find your Brother Mice."

Jumping Mouse Returned to the World of the Mice. But he Found Disappointment. No One would Listen to him. And because he was Wet, and had no Way of explaining it because there had been no Rain, many of the other Mice were Afraid of him. They believed he had been spat from the Mouth of Another Animal that had Tried to Eat him. And they all Knew that if he had not been Food for the One who Wanted him, then he must also be Poison for them.

Jumping Mouse Lived again among his People, but he could not forget his Vision of the Sacred Mountains.

The Memory burned in the Mind and Heart of Jumping Mouse, and One Day he Went to the Edge of the Place of Mice and Looked out onto the Prairie. He Looked up for Eagles. The Sky was Full of many Spots, each One an Eagle. But he was Determined to Go to the Sacred Mountains. He Gathered All of his Courage and Ran just as Fast as he Could onto the Prairie. His little Heart Pounded with Excitement and Fear.

He Ran until he Came to a Stand of Sage. He was Resting and

trying to Catch his Breath when he Saw an Old Mouse. The Patch of Sage Old Mouse Lived in was a Haven for Mice. Seeds were Plentiful and there was Nesting Material and many things to be Busy with.

"Hello," said Old Mouse. "Welcome."

Jumping Mouse was Amazed. Such a Place and such a Mouse. "You are Truly a great Mouse," Jumping Mouse said with all the Respect he could Find. "This is Truly a Wonderful Place. And the Eagles cannot See you here, either," Jumping Mouse said.

"Yes," said Old Mouse, "and One can See All the Beings of the Prairie here: the Buffalo, Antelope, Rabbit, and Coyote. One can See them All from here and Know their Names."

"That is Marvellous," Jumping Mouse said. "Can you also See the River and the Great Mountains?"

"Yes and No," Old Mouse Said with Conviction. "I Know of the Great River. But I am Afraid that the Great Mountains are only a Myth. Forget your Passion to See Them and Stay here with me. There is Everything you Want here, and it is a Good Place to Be."

"How can he Say such a thing?" Thought Jumping Mouse. "The Medicine of the Sacred Mountains is Nothing One can Forget."

"Thank you very much for the Meal you have Shared with me, Old Mouse, and also for sharing your Great Home," Jumping Mouse said. "But I must Seek the Mountains."

"You are a Foolish Mouse to Leave here. There is Danger on the Prairie! Just Look up there!" Old Mouse said, with even more Conviction. "See all those Spots! They are Eagles, and they will Catch you!"

It was hard for Jumping Mouse to Leave, but he Gathered his Determination and Ran hard Again.

The Ground was Rough. But he Arched his Tail and Ran with

All his Might. He could Feel the Shadows of the Spots upon his Back as he Ran. All those Spots! Finally he Ran into a Stand of Chokecherries. Jumping Mouse could hardly Believe his Eyes. It was Cool there and very Spacious. There was Water, Cherries and Seeds to Eat, Grasses to Gather for Nests, Holes to be Explored and many, many Other Busy Things to do. And there were a great many things to Gather.

He was Investigating his New Domain when he Heard very Heavy Breathing. He Quickly Investigated the Sound and Discovered its Source. It was a Great Mound of Hair with Black Horns. It was a Great Buffalo. Jumping Mouse could hardly Believe the Greatness of the Being he Saw Lying there before him. He was so large that Jumping Mouse could have Crawled into One of his Great Horns. "Such a Magnificent Being," Thought Jumping Mouse, and he Crept Closer.

"Hello, my Brother," said the Buffalo. "Thank you for Visiting me."

"Hello, Great Being," said Jumping Mouse. "Why are you Lying here?"

"I am Sick and I am Dying," the Buffalo said, "And my Medicine has Told me that only the Eye of a Mouse can Heal me. But little Brother, there is no such Thing as a Mouse."

Jumping Mouse was Shocked. "One of my Eyes!" he Thought, "One of my Tiny Eyes." He Scurried back into the Stand of Chokecherries. But the Breathing came Harder and Slower.

"He will Die," Thought Jumping Mouse, "If I do not Give him my Eye. He is too Great a Being to Let Die."

He Went Back to where the Buffalo Lay and Spoke. "I am a Mouse," he said with a Shaky Voice. "And you, my Brother, are a

Great Being. I cannot Let you Die. I have Two Eyes, so you may have One of them."

The minute he had Said it, Jumping Mouse's Eye Flew Out of his Head and the Buffalo was Made Whole. The Buffalo Jumped to his Feet, Shaking Jumping Mouse's Whole World.

"Thank you, my little Brother," said the Buffalo. "I Know of your Quest for the Sacred Mountains and of your Visit to the River. You have Given me Life so that I may Give-Away to the People. I will be your Brother Forever. Run under my Belly and I will Take you right to the Foot of the Sacred Mountains, and you need not Fear the Spots. The Eagles cannot See you while you Run under Me. All they will see will be the Back of a Buffalo. I am of the Prairie and I will Fall on you if I Try to Go up into the Mountains."

Little Mouse Ran under the Buffalo, Secure and Hidden from the Spots, but with only One Eye it was Frightening. The Buffalo's Great Hooves Shook the Whole World each time he took a Step. Finally they Came to a Place and Buffalo Stopped.

"This is Where I must Leave you, little Brother," said the Buffalo.

"Thank you very much," said Jumping Mouse. "But you Know, it was very Frightening Running under you with only One Eye. I was Constantly in Fear of your Great Earth-Shaking Hooves."

"Your Fear was for Nothing," said Buffalo. "For my Way of Walking is the Sun Dance Way, and I Always Know where my Hooves will Fall. I now must Return to the Prairie, my Brother. You can Always Find me there."

Jumping Mouse Immediately Began to Investigate his New Surroundings. There were even more things here than in the Other Places, Busier things, and an Abundance of Seeds and Other things Mice Like. In his Investigation of these things, Suddenly he Ran upon a Gray Wolf who was Sitting there doing absolutely Nothing.

"Hello, Brother Wolf," Jumping Mouse said.

The Wolf's Ears Came Alert and his Eyes Shone. "Wolf! Wolf! Yes, that is what I am, I am a Wolf!" But then his mind Dimmed again and it was not long before he Sat Quietly again, completely without Memory as to who he was. Each time Jumping Mouse Reminded him who he was, he became Excited with the News, but soon would Forget again.

"Such a Great Being," thought Jumping Mouse, "but he has no Memory."

Jumping Mouse Went to the Center of this New Place and was Quiet. He Listened for a very long time to the Beating of his Heart. Then Suddenly he Made up his Mind. He Scurried back to where the Wolf sat and he Spoke.

"Brother Wolf," Jumping Mouse said . . . .

"Wolf! Wolf," said the Wolf . . . .

"Please, Brother Wolf," said Jumping Mouse, "Please Listen to me. I Know what will Heal you. It is One of my Eyes. And I Want to Give it to you. I am only a Mouse. Please Take it."

When Jumping Mouse Stopped Speaking his Eye Flew out of his Head and the Wolf was made Whole.

Tears Fell down the Cheeks of Wolf, but his little Brother could not See them, for Now he was Blind.

"You are a Great Brother," said the Wolf, "for Now I have my Memory. But Now you are Blind. I am the Guide into the Sacred Mountains. I will Take you there. There is a Great Medicine Lake there. The most Beautiful Lake in the World. All the World is Reflected there. The People, the Lodges of the People, and All the Beings of the Prairies and Skies."

"Please Take me there," Jumping Mouse said.

The Wolf Guided him through the Pines to the Medicine Lake. Jumping Mouse Drank the Water from the Lake. The Wolf Described the Beauty to him.

"I must Leave you here," said Wolf, "for I must Return so that I may Guide Others, but I will Remain with you as long as you Like."

"Thank you, my Brother," said Jumping Mouse. "But although I am Frightened to be Alone, I Know you must Go so that you may Show Others the Way to this Place."

Jumping Mouse Sat there Trembling in Fear. It was no use Running, for he was Blind, but he Knew an Eagle would Find him Here. He Felt a Shadow on his Back and Heard the Sound that Eagles Make. He Braced himself for the Shock. And the Eagle Hit! Jumping Mouse went to Sleep.

Then he Woke Up. The surprise of being Alive was Great, but Now he could See! Everything was Blurry, but the Colors were Beautiful.

"I can See! I can See!" said Jumping Mouse over again and again.

A Blurry Shape Came toward Jumping Mouse. Jumping Mouse Squinted hard but the Shape remained a Blur.

"Hello, Brother," a Voice said. "Do you Want some Medicine?"

"Some Medicine for me?" asked Jumping Mouse. "Yes! Yes!"

"Then Crouch down as Low as you Can," the Voice said, "and Jump as High as you Can."

Jumping Mouse did as he was Instructed. He Crouched as Low as he Could and Jumped! The Wind Caught him and Carried him Higher.

"Do not be Afraid," the Voice called to him. "Hang on to the Wind and Trust!"

Jumping Mouse did. He Closed his Eyes and Hung on to the Wind and it Carried him Higher and Higher. Jumping Mouse Opened his Eyes and they were Clear, and the Higher he Went the Clearer they Became. Jumping Mouse Saw his Old Friend upon a Lily Pad on the Beautiful Medicine Lake. It was the Frog.

"You have a New Name," Called the Frog. "You are Eagle!"

# 6
# The Children of Hamelin: A Shamanic Journey into Mount Poppenberg

In the year 1284 a mysterious man appeared in Hameln. He was wearing a coat of many colored, bright cloth, for which reason he was called the Pied Piper. He claimed to be a rat catcher, and he promised that for a certain sum that he would rid the city of all mice and rats. The citizens struck a deal, promising him a certain price. The rat catcher then took a small fife from his pocket and began to blow on it. Rats and mice immediately came from every house and gathered around him. When he thought that he had them all he led them to the River Weser where he pulled up his clothes and walked into the water. The animals all followed him, fell in, and drowned.

Now that the citizens had been freed of their plague, they regretted having promised so much money, and, using all kinds of excuses, they refused to pay him. Finally he went away, bitter and angry. He returned on June 26, Saint John's and Saint Paul's Day, early in the morning at seven o'clock (others say it was at noon), now dressed in a hunter's costume, with a dreadful look on his face and wearing a strange red hat. He sounded his fife in the streets, but this time it wasn't rats and mice that came to him, but rather children: a great number of boys and girls from their fourth year on. Among them was the mayor's grown daughter. The swarm followed him, and he led them into a mountain, where he disappeared with them.

All this was seen by a babysitter who, carrying a child in her arms, had followed them from a distance, but had then turned around and carried the news back to the town. The anxious parents ran in droves to the town gates seeking their children. The mothers cried out and sobbed pitifully.

Within the hour messengers were sent everywhere by water and by land inquiring if the children—or any of them—had been seen, but it was all for naught.

In total, one hundred thirty were lost. Two, as some say, had lagged behind and came back. One of them was blind and the other mute. The blind one was not able to point out the place, but was able to tell how they had followed the piper. The mute one was able to point out the place, although he [or she] had heard nothing. One little boy in shirtsleeves had gone along with the others, but had turned back to fetch his jacket and thus escaped the tragedy, for when he returned, the others had already disappeared into a cave within a hill. This cave is still shown.

Until the middle of the eighteenth century, and probably still today, the street through which the children were led out to the town gate was called the bunge-lose (drumless, soundless, quiet) street, because no dancing or music was allowed there. Indeed, when a bridal procession on its way to church crossed this street, the musicians would have to stop playing. The mountain near Hameln where the children disappeared is called Poppenberg. Two stone monuments in the form of crosses have been erected there, one on the left side and one on the right. Some say that the children were led into a cave, and that they came out again in Transylvania.

The citizens of Hameln recorded this event in their town register, and they came to date all their proclamations according to the years and days since the loss of their children.

According to Seyfried the 22nd rather than the 26th of June was entered into the town register. The following lines were inscribed on the town hall:

In the year 1284 after the birth of Christ

From Hameln were led away

One hundred thirty children, born at this place

Led away by a piper into a mountain.

And on the new gate was inscribed: Centum ter denos cum magus ab urbe puellos duxerat ante annos CCLXXII condita porta fuit. [This gate was built 272 years after the magician led the 130 children from the city.]

In the year 1572 the mayor had the story portrayed in the church windows. The accompanying inscription has become largely illegible. In addition, a coin was minted in memory of the event.

Source: Jacob and Wilhelm Grimm, Die Kinder zu Hameln, Deutsche Sagen (1816/1818), vol. 1, no. 245.

\* \* \*

Despite criticism of the sexism and Christian moralizing introduced by Wilhelm into the texts of the tales they collected, from the perspective of literary history the importance of the brothers Jacob and Wilhelm Grimm cannot be overestimated. The popularity of their work in the nineteenth century acted as such a catalyst to both writers and collectors in Europe that it resulted in a veritable explosion of subsequent collections. They can also be credited with introducing the literate audience of their times to the wealth of folk and fairy tales in oral circulation, many of which, such as *The Children of Hameln* were versions of stories also found in other cultures (see Jones, 2002, p.41).

The observations of Victor Turner on the symbolic figures to be found in folk literature and on the nature of communitas are particularly pertinent when it comes to the analysis of this tale: "Folk literature abounds in symbolic figures, such as 'holy beggars,' 'third sons,' 'little tailors,' and 'simpletons,' who strip off the pretensions of holders of high rank and office and reduce them to the level of common humanity and mortality" (Turner, 1995, p.110). In the case of *The Children of Hameln*, it is of course the Pied Piper who fulfils this role, stripping off the pretensions of the citizens of the town who make false promises to him.

"In closed or structured societies it is the marginal or 'inferior' person or the 'outsider' who often comes to symbolize what David Hume has called 'the sentiment for humanity,' which in its turn relates to the model we have termed 'communitas' " (Turner, 1995, p.111). And in the closed society of Hameln, it is the Pied Piper, the outsider, who symbolizes the sentiment for humanity that the citizens of the town, in their greed and selfishness, lose sight of.

Communitas "transgresses or dissolves the norms that govern structured and institutionalized relationships and is accompanied by experiences of unprecedented potency. The processes of 'levelling' and 'stripping' ... often appear to flood their subjects with affect" (Turner, 1995, p.128). And the processes of "levelling" and "stripping" that the citizens are subjected to by the Pied Piper are used to teach them a lesson they will never forget.

Hameln is no fairytale city but a precise geographical location on the River Weser, which flows through Hamburg and into the North Sea (see Florescu, 2005, p.58). Moreover, despite the lack of genuine primary sources, the present-day version of the story is more than likely based on an actual event that can be dated back to June 26, 1284, the feast of the Apostles St.John and St.Paul. This is confirmed in what has become known as "The Luneburg Manuscript", discovered by Heinrich Spanuth, which describes the piper as a good-looking well-dressed young lad, aged about thirty, who played a silver flute. And after having assembled the 130 children, he is said to have marched them through the Eastern Gate to a location called Calvary (see Florescu, 2005, p.87). It seems that there was at least one, if not more, witnesses to the event and that search parties were sent to look for the missing children but found nothing. There is even a theory which suggests the piper was in fact Count Nicholas Von Spielenberg, a prominent member of the German aristocracy from the Hamelin area, who became "a professional recruiter, entrusted with the task of raising 130 youths for service in the Baltic lands" (Florescu, 2005, p.162). It is believed they then "perished at sea on the way to the Baltic, either attacked by pirates, hostile ships, or else by an act of God" (Florescu, 2005, p.168). However, in spite of all these findings, it is highly likely that the original version of the story *The Children of Hameln* is based on can be traced back much further, to pagan times, as will be shown.

The first question to consider is why *The Children of Hamelin* should be classified as a shamanic story. "The plot begins with the 'absence' of the shaman [in this case, the Pied Piper], opening the way to 'misfortune' [the plague of rats]" (Novik, 1989, p.57). The tale can thus be seen to have a shamanic element to it right from the very start.

It is also shamanic story in the sense that music is used to put the children into a trancelike state. They are then taken on a journey, and the mouth of the cave they are led into serves as a gateway between the two worlds. Accessing other worlds frequently involves passing through some kind of gateway, as Eliade explains:

> The "clashing of rocks," the "dancing reeds," the gates in the shape of jaws, the "two razor-edged restless mountains," the "two clashing icebergs," the "active door," the "revolving barrier," the door made of the two halves of the eagle's beak, and many more—all these are images used in myths and sagas to suggest the insurmountable difficulties of passage to the Other World (Eliade, 2003, pp.64-65).

And to make such a journey requires a change in one's mode of being, entering a transcendent state, which makes it possible to attain the world of spirit.

The shaman makes use of musical instruments such as a drum or a musical bow to help him / her (or the people he / she works with) enter an altered state of consciousness. Rattles may also be employed and sometimes shaken over the client to ascertain where the problem may lie.

It is the drum, however, that has the primary role in ceremonies in many different cultures where it is indispensable for conducting the shamanic séance, "whether it carries the shaman to the 'Center of the World,' or enables him to fly through the air, or summons and 'imprisons' the spirits, or, finally, if the drumming enables the shaman to concentrate and regain contact with the spiritual world through which he is preparing to travel" (Eliade, 1989, p.168).

It is said to be from a branch of the Cosmic Tree which stands in the Centre of the World, that the shaman makes the shell of his drum, and by the fact that it is made from this source, the shaman, through his drumming, is believed to be magically projected into the vicinity of the Tree in the Centre of the World, from where he can ascend to the sky. The drumming to call the spirits at the beginning of the séance provides the preparation for the ecstatic journey, which is probably why (among the Yakut and the Buryat) the drum was called the "shaman's horse" (see Eliade, 1989, pp.168-173).

The drum is not only spoken of as 'the shaman's horse' but also, if he has to cross water, as 'the shaman's boat'. In one case the drumstick will be his lash and the drum might be made with a horse's hide to represent the animal; in the other, the paddle for his canoe. The use of some kind of spirit boat in the shamanic journey "occurs in Siberia as well as in Malaysia and Indonesia, where it is related to the 'boat of the dead.' Often the spirit canoe is in the form of a serpent, as in aboriginal Australia, or as in the 'Snake-Canoe' of the Desana Indians of the South American tropical forest" (Harner, 1990, p.71). Another name for the drum is the 'shaman's bow', as it is known among the Yurak of the tundra. This could be because it was originally used to drive away evil spirits, when it might have served as a weapon like the archer's bow. Alternatively, it could be because the bow dispatches an arrow which flies through the air, just as the shaman is thought to fly during his journey, and an example of shamanic flight being likened to that of an arrow is that of the Greek God Apollo (see Rutherford, 1986, pp.49-50).

Neo-shamans make use of the drum for journeying too:

> A drumming tempo of about 205 to 220 beats per minute is usually effective ... Allow yourself about ten minutes

for the journey. Instruct your assistant to stop drumming at the end of ten minutes, striking the drum sharply four times to signal to you that it is time to return. Then your assistant should immediately beat the drum very rapidly for about half a minute to accompany you on the return journey, concluding with four more sharp strikes of the drum to signal that the journey is over (Harner, 1990, p.31).

Fashions change, however, and these days, would-be shamans have the option of buying "vegetarian" drums made with synthetic skins, just as there are synthetic furs.

Drumming probably facilitates shamanic states and journeying in several ways:

First, it may act as a concentration device that continuously reminds the shaman of her purpose and reduces the mind's incessant tendency to wander. It also probably drowns out other distracting stimuli and enables the shaman to focus attention inward. ... Drumming and other loud noises may also act as destabilizing factors that disrupt the ongoing psychological process by which we continuously maintain our usual state of consciousness. Charles Tart says that in his experience a sufficiently loud drumbeat feels as though it rapidly overwhelms stabilizing forces, making an abrupt change of state very easy (Walsh, 1990, pp.174-176).

There have in fact been many attempts to explain how rhythmic drumming affects us, both speculative as in the case just quoted and also more scientific efforts. Neher's (1961) investigations demonstrated that drumming could induce theta wave EEG frequency, Maxfield (1994) found that theta brain waves were synchronized with monotonous drumbeats of 3 to 6 cycles per second, and S. Harner and Tyron (1996) noted trends toward enhanced positive mood states and an increase in positive immune response to be the results of such drumming (see Krippner, 2002). Others point out that as the same shamanic states can be accessed by other means too and the healing can be affected through other forms of perceptual flooding, perhaps the use of drumming is in fact not so significant after all. Opinion remains divided and further research into the matter is clearly warranted.

What initially might appear to be unusual about *The Children of Hameln* is the musical instrument used. However, this could be due to the fact that a pipe was considered to be an instrument more familiar to the intended readership of the tale than either a shamanic drum or a musical bow would be. In Germany "people believe that by blowing the [traditional] flute [or whistle] three times one can summon the Devil or other evil spirits—one of the reasons, perhaps, why the Piper of Hamelin has often been associated with the forces of darkness" (Florescu, 2005, pp.217-218). The fact that the Pied Piper plays the Pipe could also be a reference to the woodland god Pan—Master of the Animals, the Lord of Nature, and inventor of the panpipes. And in his role as Master of the Animals, the rats would have been beings with whom it was possible for the Pied Piper both to communicate and attune himself.

The story is shamanic in another sense too, in that the Piper takes on the role of psychopomp to lead the children into what can be described as the Land of the Dead. Shamanic practitioners are uniquely suited to acting as psychopomps because of their familiarity with the terrain of the Land of the Dead. In *Shamanism: Archaic Techniques of Ecstasy*, Eliade provides an example of a Lower World journey taken by an Alaskan shaman, one of the most striking features of which is the warning not to eat food while in the Land of the Dead. There are parallels between this and the mythological tale of Hades and Persephone who, because she had been tricked into eating pomegranate seeds, was forever after unable to return fully to the world above and to her mother Demeter (see Fritz, 2003, pp.49-50).

The Land of the Dead played a significant part in the belief system of the Ancient Egyptians too, as can be seen from the texts of the so called Egyptian Book of the Dead, the *Pert em hru*, which reveal the unalterable belief of the Egyptians in the immortality of the soul, resurrection, and life after death. The sacred temple mysteries of Isis and Osiris gave initiates the opportunity to come to terms with death long before old age or disease made it obligatory to do so, and to conquer it by discovering their own immortality (see Grof, 1994, pp.9-11).

The rituals carried out by the shaman serve a similar purpose, as can be seen from how the *angakkoq*, the Greenlandic shaman, deals with the souls of the dead:

> As death is surrounded by fear the *angakkoq's* dealing with the souls of the dead is of great importance to the society. He is the mediator between the invisible world of the dead and that of the living. He is able, with the assistance of his helping spirits, to control the unpredictable consequences of the retaliation of the dead, guide the behaviour of the people involved and keep society from becoming the victim of evil forces. By his ritual death [during his initiation] he has overcome the fear of death and has thereby obtained the power of handling what is fearsome, fearlessly (Jakobsen, 1999, p.102).

In Christianity the shamanic function of psychopomp has been taken over by the priest. In Greek Orthodoxy, for example, it is believed that the soul of the dead person only departs when released by the priest at the funeral mass (see Rutherford, 1986, p.57). The same belief can actually be found in Georgian Orthodoxy too and in all its other forms—Russian, Ukrainian and so on.

What is unusual about the psychopomp in *The Children of Hameln* is the use to which he puts his skills to. However, it has to be remembered that shamans have traditionally used their powers for evil purposes at times.

In the *Shorter Oxford English Dictionary* (2002, p.2925), *a sorcerer* is defined as "A person claiming magical powers, a [practitioner of sorcery; a wizard, a magician" and there is no reference to any healing powers. The word comes from the Latin word *sortiarius*, meaning one who casts lots, or one who tells the lot of others. However, in Dan. 2:2 it is the rendering of the Hebrew *mekhashphim*, and refers to men who professed to have power with evil spirits. We also know from the Bible that the practice of sorcery resulted in severe punishment so it clearly has negative connotations. Attempts have been made to draw a distinction between someone like Carlos Castaneda, who has been labelled "a sorcerer", with its negative connotations, and shamans who do not act in such ways. It has even been suggested there is a tendency for interpreters to romantically project such features of indigenous shamanism "into otherworldly, metaphorical, meta-empirical, neutralized (or otherwise unreal) psychodrama" (Harvey, 2003, p.14). The reality is there is no such clear dividing line between the two and shamanic techniques are not always safe or necessarily conducted without malevolent designs against other persons or communities who are considered to be a threat. Lewis

(2003) refers to the Evenk Tungus shamans the Soviet ethnographer Anisimov observed, the way in which they would unleash their protective spirits on their enemies and how, in retaliation, their enemy would let loose a host of their own guardian spirits to do battle in the form of zoomorphic monsters—another example of the less palatable aspects of shamanism, as far as those who want their shamanism sanitized are concerned.

Shirokogoroff (1982) was informed by the Tungus that when the shaman goes to the Lower World, death may sometimes occur. His soul can be stopped by other spirits or even by other shamans from returning, which is why such journeys are rarely performed. This could be due to the effort made by the shaman during the performance exacerbating an already existing health problem. Another possibility could be that as he is convinced his soul cannot return, he arrests the normal functioning of the heart and the breathing himself. Either way, this provides further evidence of the dangers involved in such practices and of course, unlike packets of cigarettes, neo-shamanic workshops come with no "Government Health Warning!"

One could also refer to the Yanomamo, a tribe of Tropical Forest Indians located on the border between Venezuela and Brazil. The shamans are called *shabori* or *hekura*. The latter term is also used to signify the numerous tiny spirits they are said to have the power to manipulate. The *hekura* can be found in all sorts of places—in the hills, in trees, under rocks or even in the chest of a human. The ones considered to be "hot" and meat hungry are employed to devour the souls of enemies—especially children's souls, although they can also be used by the shamans to cure sickness. Once again, it is evident that indigenous shamanism can be a highly dangerous business.

Finally, perhaps we should consider why the Piper is described as 'Pied' as this can be another reason for classifying the tale as a shamanic one. His appearance must clearly have been striking in some way, and this was often the case with shamans when conducting rituals or ceremonies. "Everyone likes a good show and many shamans give full value for money, with impressive singing, drumming and dancing, conjuring tricks, and plenty of eye-rolling and melodramatic grimacing. However, it is the shaman's costume that really grabs the attention" (Stone, 2003, p.66). It should be pointed out that although this might well have been the case in the past, based on the accounts of the early recorders of indigenous shamanic practices, it is less applicable to what takes place in neo-shamanic circles today, where the practitioner might well be dressed in nothing more than a pair of jeans and a sweater. In fact, it is perhaps precisely because the neo-shamanic practitioner does not choose to wear a special costume that clients might turn to him in preference to a priest in a dog collar or a doctor in a white gown. What the shaman chooses to wear is really all about "horses for courses" and what works in one setting may fail dismally in another. To a large extent then, the shaman's popularity and success can be seen to depend on his sensitivity as to what will work or not, in just the same way as the success of any performer does.

Whether dressed in everyday clothes, or in a special costume, what the shaman choses to wear is calculated to act as a suggestive influence upon the minds of those he ministers to. The "magical" costume worn by shamans of old represented a religious microcosm qualitatively different from the surrounding profane space, constituting an almost complete symbolic system—a religious hierophany and cosmography. Moreover, the various objects that were attached to the costume were seen to impregnate the costume with spiritual power. Putting it on enabled the shaman to transcend profane space and prepare to enter into contact with the spiritual world (see Eliade, 1989, p.147). In other words, it acted as a prop that enabled him to enter Sacred Space.

Sometimes the costume was designed to imitate a skeleton, thus proclaiming the special status of the wearer as someone who had been dead and returned to life again. When it was in the form of a human skeleton, it is believed to have represented the family from which the ancestral shamans were successively born. Sometimes it was in the form of the skeleton of a bird. Some say the first shaman was in fact born from the union between an eagle and a woman, and the shaman himself can be regarded as a bird in the sense that, like the bird, he has access to the higher regions when he journeys to the Upper World (see Eliade, 1989, pp.159-160).

In a similar manner, the priests and ministers of religion in our own times adopt, for the most part, various modes of apparel to typify their office and the function which they perform. Liturgical vestments can be regarded as "magical" costumes, though some priests might chose not to wear them for the same reason that a neo-shamanic practitioner might choose to dress in ordinary clothes; and bread, wine, baptismal water, pulpit, and Bible serve as props for Christian worship, in just the same sense as props are used in the theatre (see Driver, 1991, p.178).

Novik suggests that shamanic legends may be classified according to three basic plot types:

> –legends about wonder-working shamans and harmful shamans ...; -legends about the competition between shamans proving strength, their battles with the evil spirits, their successful or unsuccessful attempts to obtain items

of value for themselves or for their community in the world of the spirits ...;–legends about the possibility or impossibility of people using the result achieved by the shaman for their own purposes (Novik, 1989, p.69).

According to the above classification, *The Children of Hameln* would thus belong to the third plot type in that the townsfolk can be seen to use the result achieved by the shaman (the Pied Piper) by then refusing to pay him what they had previously agreed on.

There is further evidence that points to the origins of the tale being shamanic with the Pied Piper bearing a remarkable resemblance to what is known as a *tag kizi*:

> Stories about mountain spirits who people the sacred geography of the whole Turkic world abound ... Wherever there are mountains on the planet, their beings are among the most sacred and mysterious. Part of this lies in the grandeur of the mountains themselves, and part in that they connect the earth with the sky. Mountains can be difficult to navigate and have long been home to those who wish to elude the rest of the world in caves and hidden valleys. Kotozhekov says there are two kinds of mountain beings: *tag eezi*, the actual mountain spirits; and *tag kizi*, mountain people. The latter are human beings from an earlier civilization. At one time they lived together with regular people, but then went away. They may be either our size or very large, and they have special abilities now lost by ordinary people (Deusen, 2004, pp.37-38).

Another characteristic of *tag kizi* is the way in which they are often dressed in grand but old-fashioned clothing. "In tales they often bring gifts of wealth and creativity, especially to hunters who sing and tell stories in the forest. And yet their gifts are problematical. One who receives such a gift often loses family and friends" (Deusen, 2004, p.58).

In view of the fact that the Pied Piper took the children into a mountain, that mountain could well have been his home. His power to captivate both the rats and the children would certainly seem to indicate he had special abilities, and we know from his name that he wore unusual clothing. Moreover, the gift he gave to the townsfolk, freedom from rats, clearly proved to be problematical too as it eventually led to those very same people losing their children and thus their families.

Khakassia, where mountain spirits are known as *tag eezi*, is reported to be a particularly rich source of mountain spirit lore, and apparently very similar stories are told in Tuva and other Siberian regions (see Van Deusen, 2003, p.179). We also learn, from the same source, that in many Khakassian tales mountain spirits are described with details of their rich clothing, that their homes are often reached by hidden openings in rocks (which is where the Pied Piper takes the children), and that spirits may abduct human beings, sometimes permanently, as the Pied Piper does (see Van Deusen, 2003, pp.181-182). As for the connection between mountain spirits and shamans, they give information by means of divination as the Pied Piper can be said to provide the townspeople with, and they sometimes lure people to their death, once again as the Pied Piper does (see Van Deusen, 2003, p.187).

Interestingly, however, "of the shamanic repertoire, only soul retrieval seems to be absent in mountain spirit lore. These spirits do not engage in healing … Mountain spirits act from the side of the dead, not the living– pointing up the moments of choice" (Van Deusen, 2003, p.188). Once again this is evident in *The Children of Hameln* in that at the end of the tale the problem of the missing children remains unresolved and the townspeople are left to live with the choice they made.

As to whether the similarity between the Pied Piper and the *tag kizi* indicates diffusion from a common source, the recurrence of a universal archetype figure deeply buried in the human psyche, or simply the writer of this thesis exhibiting a common human aptitude for resorting to analogy, there is unfortunately no way of knowing for sure. To make out a convincing case for there being a definite connection between the *tag kizi* and the Pied Piper, and to avoid the risk of error inherent in comparative studies based on the single criterion of resemblance, one would need to find a Turkic version of the Pied Piper tale, which to date has not been possible.

Moreover, in view of the fact that "it is well-known, and amply borne out by the errors of comparative mythology, that ... resemblances can be extremely deceptive", and to avoid the danger inherent in "comparative studies based on the single criterion of resemblance" (Lévi-Strauss, 1981, pp.37-38), no further conjecture on this matter is likely to be helpful until (or unless) further concrete evidence can be unearthed to support such a claim.

There are of course good reasons for retelling a tale in such a manner that it seems for its audience and readers, closer to home than the original; in other words, to give it a local rather than a "foreign" setting. This has been an established literary device in all cultures and at all times. Indeed, this could well have been what happened to *The Children of Hameln* which, as we have shown, is more than likely based on a much earlier shamanic tale and is possibly of Turkic origins.

Although it has been claimed that myths of a given population can only be interpreted and understood in the framework of the culture of that given population, neighbouring populations have surely always, to some extent, been aware of what was going on in the other population. Coupled with this is the argument that we have a shared innate propensity to conjure up images of certain archetypal figures, however geographically distant we may be from each other. Giving further support to the argument in favour of comparing culturally diverse stories is Winkleman's suggestion that the fundamental similarities across time, space, and cultures in the phenomena of shamanism indicate these traditions develop from a common psychobiological basis. He cites as proof the way in which the characteristics of the !Kung Bushman Num master in twentieth century Africa are strikingly similar to the characteristics of the classic descriptions of the Siberian shaman (see Winkelman, 2000, p.71).

Consequently, the attempt to find connections between shamanic stories from different cultures, as we have been doing here, can in fact be justified to a certain extent.

What takes place in the story on a mass scale can be regarded as a case of both body and soul theft, caused by the sins of the townsfolk, who refuse to keep their promise to pay the Piper what they initially agreed on. One is reminded of Bunyan's sermon, *The Greatness of the Soul: And the Unspeakableness of the Loss thereof*, referred to previously in the Introduction.

Bunyan sees the cause of soul-loss as being sin and quotes from the Bible to support his case:

The cause is laid down in the 18th chapter of Ezekiel, in

these words: Behold, all souls, says God, are Mine; as the soul of the father, so also the soul of the son is Mine: the soul that sinneth, it shall die (5:4). ... It is sin, then, or sinning against God, that is the cause of dying, or damning in hell fire, for that must be meant by dying; otherwise, to die, according to our ordinary acceptation of the notion, the soul is not capable of, it being indeed immortal, as hath been afore asserted. So, then, the soul that sinneth, that is, and persevering in the same that soul shall die, be cast away, or damned; yea, to ascertain us of the undoubted truth of this, the Holy Ghost doth repeat it again, and that in this very chapter, saying, The soul that sinneth, it shall die (5:20) (Bunyan, 1845, p.53).

The solution Bunyan proposed was to instil transgressors or potential transgressors with fear of damnation to encourage them to change their ways. And in *The Children of Hameln*, the fear of losing what is most precious to most parents, their children, serves to promote the kind of values most good Christians would aspire to.

Florescu suggests *The Children of Hameln* "is still exploited as a moral tale in the best tradition of La Fontaine, to instil ethical standards among ill-disciplined young people; you must obey the rules established by society, particularly the keeping of promises, or else the Devil will take you away" (Florescu, 2005, p.237).

The idea of frightening disobedient children into behaving is a common occurrence in folktales, with *Little Red Riding Hood* providing a good example in that she is punished for disobeying her mother. The Germans refer to such tales as *schreckmärchen* (scare-tales). And Ashliman describes an unusual statue that can be found in Bern, Switzerland, which serves the same purpose:

High on a pedestal at the *Kornhausplatz*, in the center of the old city, stands an ogre, *der Chindlifrässer*, surrounded by terrified children. He has captured half a dozen children. They are in his pockets and arms, all awaiting the fate of the one whose head he has taken entirely into his mouth. Since about 1545 this statue has graphically warned Swiss children of the potentially dire consequences of disobedience (taken from Ashliman, D.L. *Aging and Death in Folklore* http://www.pitt.edu [accessed 24/01/2005]).

However, in view of the fact that it is clearly the adults who fail to keep their promises in *The Children of Hameln* and the children would appear to do nothing wrong at all, it is questionable whether it actually provides a good example of the kind of tale Florescu and Ashliman both refer to.

On the other hand, it is possible to agree with Florescu when he suggests that the departure of the children, led by the piper playing his flute, to a mountainside from which there is no return can be said to represent "an initiation rite, still practised in our time by all societies marking the passage from childhood to adulthood" (Florescu, 2005, p.238). Indeed, Appollo Smintheus, who was known as the protector of rats, was also in his Greek appearance, a musician who, like the Piper, presided over the initiation rites of young men (see Florescu, 2005, p.216). It thus becomes apparent that what we have in *The Children of Hameln* is analogous to a palimpsest, with the deeper, older strata of shamanic imagery detectable in fragments through the dominant, later Christian overlay (see Metzner, 1999, p.121).

Further evidence to support the case for this argument can be found in the fact that the feast of the Apostles St. John and St. Paul, which is when the historic event the present-day version of the story probably took place, coincided with the summer solstice, celebrating the longest night of the year, which can be traced back to pagan times. In medieval Germany the festivities usually extended over a period of six days and "One rite often performed in northern Germany was for a youth called the Marcher to play some sort of magical tune, with his feet in the water or on the edge of a forest. As the reincarnation of an evil spirit, he would steal away the souls of all those who dared to approach him" (Florescu, 2005, p.123). It should be born in mind that in Hameln, as elsewhere in Europe during this period of time, childhood was considered to extend from babyhood through to puberty and could even include single people as old as twenty. Thus the "children" lured by the piper could well have been a lot older than we imagine them to have been.

According to deconstructionists, polarities and privileged positions are simply arbitrary human constructions, and "objective reality" does not exist (see Hansen, 2001, p. 64). Shamans can be regarded as master deconstructionalists as by consorting with spirits, for example, they regularly deconstruct the polarity of life and death. One can even argue it is essential for shamans to deconstruct order, especially if a person's or a community's rigidity of outlook have blocked adaptation and growth, and they need to view their situation in a new light in order to remove the impasse. The piper, in the role of shaman, can be said to deconstruct the order in the lives of the townsfolk by stealing the souls of their children and so teaching them a lesson they will never forget.

"[In] any story which is completely resolved, the basic pattern remains the same. In the end, darkness is overcome and light wins the day" (Booker, 2004, p.219). However, when the soul is not recovered (or, as in this case, the souls are not recovered) there is clearly no such resolution and darkness remains.

In conclusion, what Victor Turner has to say about the nature of social dramas in particularly relevant to the ending of this particular tale:

[W]hen conflict emerges from the opposed interests and claims of protagonists acting under a single social principle ... judicial institutions can be invoked to meet the crisis, for a rational attempt can be made to adjust claims that are similarly based. But when claims are advanced under different social principles, which are inconsistent with one another even to the point of mutual contradiction, [such as is the case between the Pied Piper and Hameln's officials] there can be no rational settlement (Turner, 1982, p.75).

A common feature of shamanic stories is an etiological finale, one which relates "an event in the account to the present state of affairs ... an explanation of the current state of elements in the natural world and the culture" (Novik, 1989, p.31). Such a finale may pertain to the history of a particular sacred place or ritual object or "the expounding of a moral lesson, the explanation of fortunes or misfortunes that have become 'ever since then' the lot of the narrator or his relatives" (Novik, 1989, p.31). In the case of *The Children of Hameln*, it is a moral lesson that is expounded, warning us of the consequences that await if we dare to break our promises as the townsfolk did.

# References

Booker, C. (2004) *The Seven Basic Plots: Why we tell Stories*, London: Continuum.

Bunyan, J. (1845) *The Greatness of the Soul: And the Unspeakableness of the Loss thereof*, London: Thomas Nelson (first published in 1682).

Deusen, K.V. (2004) *Healing Drum: Shamans and Storytellers of Turkic Siberia*, Seattle: University of Washington Press.

Driver, T.F. (1991) *The Magic of Ritual*, New York: Harper Collins Publishers.

Eliade, M. (1989) *Shamanism: Archaic techniques of ecstasy*, London: Arkana (first published in the USA by Pantheon Books 1964).

—. (2003) *Rites and Symbols of Initiation*, Putnam, Connecticut: Spring Publications (originally published by Harper Bros., New York, 1958).

Florescu, R. (2005) *In Search of the Pied Piper*, London: Athena Press.

Fritz, F.J. (2003) *Shamanic Psychopomp: Guide of Souls*, USA: 1st Books Library.

Grof, S. (1994) *Books of the Dead: Manuals for Living and Dying*, London: Thames & Hudson.

Hansen, G. P. (2001) *The Trickster and the Paranormal*, New York: Xlibris.

Harner, M. (1990 3rd Edition) *The Way of the Shaman*, Harper & Row (first

published by Harper & Row in 1980).

Harner, S., & Tyron, W. (1996) 'Psychological and immunological responses to shamanic journeying with drumming.' *Shaman, 4*, 89-97.

Harvey, G. (ed.) (2003) *Shamanism: A Reader*, London: Routledge.

Jakobsen, M.D. (1999) *Shamanism: Traditional and Contemporary*

*Approaches to the Mastery of Spirits and Healing*, New York & Oxford: Berghahn Books.

Jones, S.S. (2002) *The Fairy Tale: The Magic Mirror of Imagination*, London: Routledge.

Krippner, S.C. 'Conflicting Perspectives on Shamans and Shamanism: Points and Counterpoints'. www.stanleykrippner.com/papers/conflicting_perspectives.htm [accessed 31/3/05].

Lévi-Strauss, C. (1981) *Introduction to a science of mythology - 4: The naked man*,

London: Cape, 1981.

Lewis, I.M. (2003 3rd Edition) *Ecstatic Religion: a study of shamanism and spirit*

*possession*, London: Routledge (first published 1971 by Penguin Books).

Metzner, R. (1999) *Green Psychology: Transforming Our Relationship to the Earth*, Rochester, Vermont: Park Street Press.

Novik, E.S. (1979) 'Struktura shamanskikh deistv' in Baiburin, A.K. & Chistov, K.V. (eds.) *Problemy slavianskoi etnografii*, Leningrad: Nauka.

—. (1989) 'The Archaic Epic and Its Relationship to Ritual.' In *Soviet Anthropology and Archeology* FALL 1989/VOL. 28, NO. 2. S.20-100.

Rutherford, W. (1986) *Shamanism: the foundations of magic*, Wellingborough Northamptonshire: The Aquarius Press.

Shirokogoroff, S.M. (1982) *Psychomental Complex of the Tungus*, London: Keegan Paul Trench, Trubner & Co., Ltd. (first published in 1935).

Stone, A. (2003) *Explore Shamanism*, UK: Loughborough: Heart of Albion Press.

Turner, V. (1982) *From Ritual to Theatre: The Human Seriousness of Play*, New York: PAJ Publications (A division of Performing Arts Journal, Inc.).

Turner, V. (1995) *The Ritual Process: Structure and Anti-Structure*, Chicago, Illinois: Aldine Publishing Company (first published in 1969).

Van Deusen, K. 'Khakassian Mountain Spirit and Snake Lore.' In *Shaman* Volume 11 Nos. 1-2 Spring and Autumn 2003.

Walsh, R. N. (1990) *The Spirit of Shamanism*, London: Mandala.

Winkelman, M. (2000) *Shamanism: The Neural Ecology of Consciousness and Healing*, Westport, Connecticut: Bergin & Garvey.

# 7
# The Crystal Clear Waters of Mount Elbruz

Versions of the Prometheus saga can be found throughout the Caucasus as it was to Mount Elbruz that the figure from Greek mythology, was chained. He was exiled to the Caucasus for disobeying the Gods by bringing fire to mankind. The variant presented below is Kabardian and was taken from *Georgian Folk Tales*, translated by Marjorie Wardrop. The Kabardians are Circassians, and Kabardino-Cherkess is an Adyga language which is spoken in the Kabardino-Balkaria autonomous region of the north-west Caucasus between Karachay-Cherkessia and North Ossetia.

> "The first reference to Circassians in English dates from 1555. Thereafter the term became the equivalent of the Russian *gortsy*, a blanket label for virtually any exotic Eurasian highlander, whether dark or fair, caftaned or trousered, noble or commoner" (King, 2008, p.92). However, what Circassian (Russ. *cherkes*, Turk, *Çerkez*) refers to in its narrowest sense is speakers of Adyga languages, the major linguistic group of the region.

The people who inhabit the region are Moslems, "but with significant remaining traces of Christianity and paganism, even to the present day" (Hunt, 2004, p.9).

**Conference of Circassian princes in 1839-40**

From the album 'Le Concaseploresque. Dessin d'après nature par le Prince G.Gagarin', Paris, 1847. Scanned from pdf-file Оружие Народов Кавказа of E.G. Astvatsaturyan, St. Petersburg: Atlant, 2004. Located on the website «Encyclopedic Album of Circassian weapon» (www.nartalbum.com) Grigory Gagarin (1811-1893)

# The Prometheus saga – a Kabardian variant

A long, long time ago, a certain giant who had one eye in the middle of his forehead dared to penetrate into the secrets with which God had surrounded the summit of Mount Elbruz. He came to the saddle between the two peaks, from the rocks at the foot of which a well of crystal clear water springs up. But God would not permit that, and chained the violator of His secrets with a long chain to the rocks.

Many years have passed since then. The giant has grown old. His long beard reaches to his knees; his once mighty frame has become bent and his proud countenance is covered with wrinkles. To punish him still more God sent a bird of prey, which lies up every day to peck at the giant's heart. And when the tormented giant bends forward to drink, the bird swoops down and sucks up the water down to the last drop. The water of that spring has a wonderful power; whosoever drinks of it will live forever.

But a time will come when God will be angry with the sons of Adam. Then He will set the one-eyed giant free, and woe betide mankind. For he will wreak vengeance on them for his long sufferings.

\* \* \*

Writers of all ranks, from belletrists to the titans of the Russian literary canon, have found inspiration in the Caucasus as a subject and a setting, including Lermentov, Pushkin, and Tolstoy. John Steinbeck can be included among their number too. During a visit in the late 1940s, he described it as "a magical place" and one that "becomes dream-like the moment you have left it" (see King, 2008, p.206). And anyone who has visited the region will have no hesitation in confirming this as it undoubtedly does leave you with the impression that you have been to another reality and back.

As for the waters, they have been described as the reservoir of all the potentialities of existence because they not only precede every form but they also serve to sustain every creation. Immersion is equivalent to dissolution of form, in other words death, whereas emergence repeats the cosmogonic act of formal manifestation, in other words re-birth (see Eliade, 1952, p.151).

As Eliade points out, in whatever religious context we find it, water invariably serves the function of dissolving the forms of things, and it can be seen to be both purifying and regenerative. "The purpose of the ritual lustrations and purifications is to gain a flash of realisation of the non-temporal moment ... in which the creation took place; they are symbolical repetitions of the birth of worlds or of the 'new man'." (Eliade, 1952, p.152).

The idea of regeneration through water can be found in numerous pan-cultural tales about the miraculous Fountain of Youth. So pervasive were these legends that in the 16th century the Spanish conquistador Ponce de Leon actually set out to find it once and for all — and found Florida instead. In Japanese legends, the white and yellow leaves of the wild chrysanthemum confer blessings from Kiku-Jido, the chrysanthemum boy who dwells by the Fountain of Youth. These leaves are ceremonially dipped in sake to assure good health and long life. One Native American story describes the Fountain of Youth created by two hawks in the nether-world between heaven and earth. Those who drink of it outlive their children and friends, which is why it is eventually destroyed.

What follows is a guided visualisation based on the story presented above. If you are working on your own, it is suggested that you record the script, perhaps with some appropriate background music. You can then lie somewhere comfortable, where you will not be disturbed, and play the recording back to yourself as you go through the process described.

# The healing power of water

*Script for the guide:* (To be read in a gentle trance-inducing voice). Make yourself comfortable and close your eyes. Take a few deep breaths to help you relax. Feel the tension disappear stage by stage from the top of your head to the tips of your toes. Let your surroundings fade away as you gradually sink backwards through time and actuality and pass through the gateway of this reality into the dreamtime. (When the participants are fully relaxed, begin the next stage).

You find yourself standing at the foot of the two peaks of Mount Elbruz, a place of power, where many have come before you for, and where many will no doubt come after you. And you know, whatever your problem is, that it is here you will find help, and that is what has brought you to this place.

Ahead of you there's a winding path, leading up to the summit. The climb is steep but you're determined and refuse to be deterred. And the higher you climb, the stronger your resolve becomes, the resolve you have to achieve what you have set out to do.

Eventually you come to the saddle between the two peaks of the mountain, where, from the rocks, a well of crystal clear water springs up. And, as you know, the water of this spring has a wonderful power; whosoever drinks of it will live forever in that their spirit for enjoying and making the most of life will be rekindled and never die again. This is the moment you have been waiting for.

And, as you stoop down low to cup the water in your hands and savour it, take a minute of clock time, equal to all the time you need, to appreciate the renewed spirit it fills you with, like liquid crystal running through your veins …

And you know now, with an unfailing certainty, such as you have never experienced before, that never again will life seem to be nothing more than a chore to you, that never again will you feel that you can't go on. For, refreshed and revitalised, you know now that you will never grow tired of life again, and that as a result, you are now able to act and move forward once again. So take a minute of clock time, equal to all the time you need, to reflect on what it is you have blessed with today …

And now that the purpose of your journey has been accomplished, now that your spirit has been rekindled, the time has come to make your way back home, back, back, down the side of the mountain, back, down to the base where you stood at the start of your journey and back on to the track that leads you to your home, back, back, back to the start of your new life and back to the place you started from.

Take a deep breath, let it all out slowly, open your eyes, and smile at the first person you see. Stretch your arms, stretch your legs, stamp your feet on the ground, and make sure you're really back, back in …, back where you started from. Welcome home!

Now take a few minutes in silence to make some notes on the experiences you had on your journeys, which you can then share with the rest of the group.

Or

Now take a few minutes in silence to make some notes on the experiences you had on your journeys, which you can then make a note of in your dream journal.

Or

And now you might like to turn to the person sitting next to you and share some of the experiences you had on your journeys.

# References

Berman, M. (2011) *Guided Visualisations through the Caucasus*, California: Pendraig Publishing.

Eliade, M. (1991) *Images and Symbols*, New Jersey: Princeton University Press (The original edition is copyright Librairie Gallimard 1952).

Hunt, D.G. (2004) *Folklore of the North-West Caucasus and Chechnya*, Tbilisi: Caucasus House.

King, C. (2008) *The Ghost of Freedom*, New York: Oxford University Press Inc.

Wardrop, M. (1894) *Georgian Folk Tales*, London: David Nutt

# 8

# The Vision Quest, Mount Sinai, and a Dream Fulfilled

In many Native American groups, what is known as the vision quest is a rite of passage – a turning point in life taken before puberty to find oneself and the intended spiritual and life direction. When an older child is ready, he or she will go on a personal, spiritual quest alone in the wilderness, often in conjunction with a period of fasting. This usually lasts for a number of days while the child is attuned to the spirit world. Usually, a Guardian animal will come in a vision or dream, and the child's life direction will appear at some point. After a vision quest, the child returns to the tribe and may become an apprentice so as to learn how to follow the path that was indicated.

To induce a heightened state of awareness in the initiate and to enable him or her to have visions, sensory deprivation methods may be employed. This can include nights spent alone on a mountain or in a wilderness area, fasting, sleep deprivation, or being enclosed in a small room (e.g. igloo).

Vision quests can also be undertaken at other turning points in our lives, and it can be argued that the ascent of Mount Sinai by Moses represents one such example. Mount Sinai, also known as

Mount Horeb or Mount Musa, is the name of a mountain near Saint Catherine in the Sinai Peninsula of Egypt. According to Jewish, Christian and Islamic tradition, Mount Sinai is the place where Moses received the Ten Commandments, though not all parties agree that it is this particular mountain, which was mentioned in the Bible.

The earliest Christian traditions place this event at the nearby Mount Serbal, and a monastery was founded at its base in the 4th century; it was only in the 6th century that the monastery moved to the foot of Mount Catherine, following the guidance of Josephus' earlier claim that Sinai was the highest mountain in the area. Jebel Musa, which is adjacent to Mount Catherine, was only equated with Sinai, by Christians, after the 15th century.

Many modern biblical scholars now believe that the Israelites would have crossed the Sinai peninsula in a straight line, rather than detouring to the southern tip (assuming that they did not cross the eastern branch of the Red Sea in boats or on a sandbar), and therefore look for Mount Sinai elsewhere.

The Song of Deborah, which textual scholars consider to be one of the oldest parts of the Bible, suggests that Yahweh dwelt at Mount Seir, so many scholars favour a location in Nabatea (modern Arabia). Alternatively, the biblical descriptions of Sinai can be interpreted as describing a volcano, and so a small number of scholars have considered equating Sinai with locations in northwestern Saudi Arabia as there are no volcanoes in the Sinai Peninsula.

For Muslims, there is a chapter, which mentions the mountain in the Qur'an, entitled Surat At-Tin, surah 95, in which Allah swears by the fig and the olive, by Mount Sinai, and by the city of Mecca. Muslims also consider the depression below Mount Sinai, known as "Tuwa", to be sacred as mentioned in the Qur'an as the "Holy Valley."

The Ten Commandments, illustration from a Bible card published by the Providence Lithograph Company 1907 - Wikipedia

The verses in the Qur'an that mention Mount Sinai are verse 23:20, verse 2:63, verse 52:1, verse 95:2, verse 4:154, verse 28:29, and verse 7:171.

According to the biblical account, after leaving Egypt and crossing the Red Sea, the Israelites arrived at the foot of the holy mountain and gathered there in anticipation of the words of God. Even prior to this, the mountain was considered holy as Moses encountered the burning bush upon the same mountain (called Horeb in the first instance). And what is reputed to be the very same bush that Moses witnessed can be seen in the grounds of the monastery even today.

In fact, sacred mountains are often seen as sites of revelation and inspiration. Mount Tabor, for example, is where it is supposed Jesus was revealed to be the son of God, and Muhammed is said to have received his first revelation on Mount Hira.

As one of the most sacred mountains in the Middle East, and one of the few sacred places arguably equally revered by Jews, Christians, and Muslims, Mount Sinai is also a popular location for pilgrimages. One route, called the Steps of Repentance, is composed of 3,000 steps that were carved into the mountainside by a monk. Various sights mentioned in the Old Testament can be seen on the mountain's summit too, such as the area where Moses "sheltered from the total glory of God".

The passages from the Old Testament that refer to the gathering of the Israelites at the foot of the mountain and Moses' ascent are presented below in full, and these are followed first by a parallel etiological tale from the Philippines, and then by a contemporary story that takes its inspiration from the biblical account:

# King James Version: Exodus Chapter 19

1 In the third month, when the children of Israel were gone forth out of the land of Egypt, the same day came they into the wilderness of Sinai.

2 For they were departed from Rephidim, and were come to the desert of Sinai, and had pitched in the wilderness; and there Israel camped before the mount.

3 And Moses went up unto God, and the LORD called unto him out of the mountain, saying, Thus shalt thou say to the house of Jacob, and tell the children of Israel;

4 Ye have seen what I did unto the Egyptians, and how I bare you on eagles' wings, and brought you unto myself.

5 Now therefore, if ye will obey my voice indeed, and keep my covenant, then ye shall be a peculiar treasure unto me above all people: for all the earth is mine:

6 And ye shall be unto me a kingdom of priests, and a holy nation. These are the words which thou shalt speak unto the children of Israel.

7 And Moses came and called for the elders of the people, and laid before their faces all these words which the LORD commanded him.

8 And all the people answered together, and said, All that the LORD hath spoken we will do. And Moses returned the words of the people unto the LORD.

9 And the LORD said unto Moses, Lo, I come unto thee in a thick cloud, that the people may hear when I speak with thee, and believe thee for ever. And Moses told the words of the people unto the LORD.

10 And the LORD said unto Moses, Go unto the people, and sanctify them to day and tomorrow, and let them wash their clothes,

11 And be ready against the third day: for the third day the LORD will come down in the sight of all the people upon mount Sinai.

12 And thou shalt set bounds unto the people round about, saying, Take heed to yourselves, that ye go not up into the mount, or touch the border of it: whosoever toucheth the mount shall be surely put to death:

13 There shall not an hand touch it, but he shall surely be stoned, or shot through; whether it be beast or man, it shall not live: when the trumpet soundeth long, they shall come up to the mount.

14 And Moses went down from the mount unto the people, and sanctified the people; and they washed their clothes.

15 And he said unto the people, Be ready against the third day: come not at your wives.

16 And it came to pass on the third day in the morning, that there were thunders and lightnings, and a thick cloud upon the mount, and the voice of the trumpet exceeding

loud; so that all the people that was in the camp trembled.

17 And Moses brought forth the people out of the camp to meet with God; and they stood at the nether part of the mount.

18 And mount Sinai was altogether on a smoke, because the LORD descended upon it in fire: and the smoke thereof ascended as the smoke of a furnace, and the whole mount quaked greatly.

19 And when the voice of the trumpet sounded long, and waxed louder and louder, Moses spake, and God answered him by a voice.

20 And the LORD came down upon mount Sinai, on the top of the mount: and the LORD called Moses up to the top of the mount; and Moses went up.

21 And the LORD said unto Moses, Go down, charge the people, lest they break through unto the LORD to gaze, and many of them perish.

22 And let the priests also, which come near to the LORD, sanctify themselves, lest the LORD break forth upon them.

23 And Moses said unto the LORD, The people cannot come up to mount Sinai: for thou chargedst us, saying, Set bounds about the mount, and sanctify it.

24 And the LORD said unto him, Away, get thee down, and thou shalt come up, thou, and Aaron with thee: but let

not the priests and the people break through to come up unto the LORD, lest he break forth upon them.

25 So Moses went down unto the people, and spake unto them.

---

# King James Version: Exodus Chapter 34

1 And the LORD said unto Moses, Hew thee two tables of stone like unto the first: and I will write upon these tables the words that were in the first tables, which thou brakest.

2 And be ready in the morning, and come up in the morning unto mount Sinai, and present thyself there to me in the top of the mount.

3 And no man shall come up with thee, neither let any man be seen throughout all the mount; neither let the flocks nor herds feed before that mount.

4 And he hewed two tables of stone like unto the first; and Moses rose up early in the morning, and went up unto mount Sinai, as the LORD had commanded him, and took in his hand the two tables of stone.

5 And the LORD descended in the cloud, and stood with him there, and proclaimed the name of the LORD.

6 And the LORD passed by before him, and proclaimed, The LORD, The LORD God, merciful and gracious,

longsuffering, and abundant in goodness and truth,

7 Keeping mercy for thousands, forgiving iniquity and transgression and sin, and that will by no means clear the guilty; visiting the iniquity of the fathers upon the children, and upon the children's children, unto the third and to the fourth generation.

8 And Moses made haste, and bowed his head toward the earth, and worshipped.

9 And he said, If now I have found grace in thy sight, O LORD, let my LORD, I pray thee, go among us; for it is a stiffnecked people; and pardon our iniquity and our sin, and take us for thine inheritance.

10 And he said, Behold, I make a covenant: before all thy people I will do marvels, such as have not been done in all the earth, nor in any nation: and all the people among which thou art shall see the work of the LORD: for it is a terrible thing that I will do with thee.

11 Observe thou that which I command thee this day: behold, I drive out before thee the Amorite, and the Canaanite, and the Hittite, and the Perizzite, and the Hivite, and the Jebusite.

12 Take heed to thyself, lest thou make a covenant with the inhabitants of the land whither thou goest, lest it be for a snare in the midst of thee:

13 But ye shall destroy their altars, break their images, and cut down their groves:

14 For thou shalt worship no other god: for the LORD, whose name is Jealous, is a jealous God:

15 Lest thou make a covenant with the inhabitants of the land, and they go a whoring after their gods, and do sacrifice unto their Gods, and one call thee, and thou eat of his sacrifice;

16 And thou take of their daughters unto thy sons, and their daughters go a whoring after their gods, and make thy sons go a whoring after their Gods.

17 Thou shalt make thee no molten Gods.

18 The feast of unleavened bread shalt thou keep. Seven days thou shalt eat unleavened bread, as I commanded thee, in the time of the month Abib: for in the month Abib thou camest out from Egypt.

19 All that openeth the matrix is mine; and every firstling among thy cattle, whether ox or sheep, that is male.

20 But the firstling of an ass thou shalt redeem with a lamb: and if thou redeem him not, then shalt thou break his neck. All the firstborn of thy sons thou shalt redeem. And none shall appear before me empty.

21 Six days thou shalt work, but on the seventh day thou shalt rest: in earing time and in harvest thou shalt rest.

22 And thou shalt observe the feast of weeks, of the firstfruits of wheat harvest, and the feast of ingathering at the year's end.

23 Thrice in the year shall all your menchildren appear before the LORD God, the God of Israel.

24 For I will cast out the nations before thee, and enlarge thy borders: neither shall any man desire thy land, when thou shalt go up to appear before the LORD thy God thrice in the year.

25 Thou shalt not offer the blood of my sacrifice with leaven; neither shall the sacrifice of the feast of the passover be left unto the morning.

26 The first of the firstfruits of thy land thou shalt bring unto the house of the LORD thy God. Thou shalt not seethe a kid in his mother's milk.

27 And the LORD said unto Moses, Write thou these words: for after the tenor of these words I have made a covenant with thee and with Israel.

28 And he was there with the LORD forty days and forty nights; he did neither eat bread, nor drink water. And he wrote upon the tables the words of the covenant, the ten commandments.

29 And it came to pass, when Moses came down from mount Sinai with the two tables of testimony in Moses' hand, when he came down from the mount, that Moses

wist not that the skin of his face shone while he talked with him.

30 And when Aaron and all the children of Israel saw Moses, behold, the skin of his face shone; and they were afraid to come nigh him.

31 And Moses called unto them; and Aaron and all the rulers of the congregation returned unto him: and Moses talked with them.

32 And afterward all the children of Israel came nigh: and he gave them in commandment all that the LORD had spoken with him in mount Sinai.

33 And till Moses had done speaking with them, he put a veil on his face.

34 But when Moses went in before the LORD to speak with him, he took the veil off, until he came out. And he came out, and spake unto the children of Israel that which he was commanded.

35 And the children of Israel saw the face of Moses, that the skin of Moses' face shone: and Moses put the veil upon his face again, until he went in to speak with him.

\* \* \*

In addition to the biblical account, there are many other versions of the story, and the one that follows comes from the Philippines:

# Why There Are Many Languages On Earth

When the people heard that the rice Dakbungan had planted had come from heaven, some of them wanted to go to heaven too. However, they did not know how Dakbungan got there, so they decided to build a stairway that would take them there.

For many days the people toiled. After a few weeks, the stairway measured taller than a house, but it was still not high enough to reach heaven. After a few months, the stairway was just as high as some of the nearby mountains but still, it could not take the people to heaven.

One day, when the gods looked upon the earth, they saw the stairway and the people busily labouring over it. They said to each other, "Look! The people are trying to reach heaven. This will not do. They're wasting their time. And look at how deserted their villages are. We must put a stop to this."

The gods created lightning and threw the lightning bolts down through the sky. The people at work on the stairway were frightened, for they had never seen lightning bolts before. "Run!" they cried. "What sort of giant spears are these? They seem to be made of fire! The gods must be angry!"

In great haste they scrambled down the stairway to seek cover among the bushes and rocks, babbling words they suddenly could not understand. Each of the men had begun to speak a different language.

When all was quiet once more, the men came out of hiding. They had forgotten all about the stairway to heaven, and now they were tired and hungry. One said, "Idawis tako ta styay man-is."

Another said, "Ayshi may kekdot et mango say en amis." Another said, "Let's roast our food on a good fire." Still another said, "Saan,

Sermon On The Mount Carl Bloch (1834–1890)

ituno tayo tapno naimas."

All of them began to speak at the same time, not knowing that they all meant the same thing.

Not being able to understand each other, all of them soon went off to their own villages. As for the stairway, it was never finished since the people no longer spoke in the same tongue.

* * *

## The Child of God

The pre-ordained date finally came round again and everyone gathered in a circle at the foot of the Sacred Mountain, waiting for the sun to rise and the long-anticipated Ceremony to commence.

The people came from far and wide and from all walks of life. But what all the couples shared was a common purpose – to be present for the Allocation Ceremony at which the newly born would be handed out.

Khatuna was late as usual. She'd got side-tracked along the way, stopping to help out an elderly compatriot who'd injured himself in a fall. So by the time Khatuna and her man reached the site, all the babies had already been allocated, all the couples had already been dispersed, and God was already packing his bags and making preparations for his journey home.

Khatuna and Irakli were devastated. They'd been waiting all year for this day to come round and now they'd missed their one and only chance.

God was distressed too for he knew how much this day had meant to them and of all the trouble they had gone to in order to obtain the necessary paperwork to attend.

"I just wish there was something I could do to help you both," God sighed. "But I can't give you what I haven't got."

Mount Sinai - Wikipedia
Yerevan, Armenia - with the backdrop of Mount Ararat

"Please God. There must be something you can do." Khatuna pleaded. "I know it's not for us to judge who's worthy to be a parent. But who knows us better than we know ourselves, you who watch over us as we go about our daily tasks, must surely be aware of how committed we are to parenthood and how seriously we would take our duties, were we to be given the chance."

"Well, to be completely honest with you, there is one child left. But he was born prematurely so I put him to one side."

Without any hesitation, Khatuna boldly stepped forward and staked her claim. "Our love and dedication will provide the child with all he could possibly need to develop and thrive."

"Yes. I truly believe it will. Take the infant with my blessing. But there's one condition attached," God added. "Don't turn to look back on me after you leave. For, if you do so, then all will be lost."

It was not for Khatuna and Irakli to question their Lord and of course they followed his instructions to the letter.

But what if they had looked back? If they had, they would have seen God crying because he'd entrusted to their safekeeping his one and only son.

\* \* \*

Any consideration of the ascent of Mount Sinai by Moses would be incomplete without mention of Jesus and the Sermon on the Mount - a collection of sayings and teachings of Jesus, which emphasizes his moral teaching found in the Canonical Gospel of Matthew. According to chapters 5-7, Jesus of Nazareth gave this sermon (estimated around AD 30) on a mountainside to his disciples and a large crowd.

The best-known written portions of the sermon comprise the Beatitudes, found at the beginning of the section. The sermon also contains the Lord's Prayer and the injunctions "resist not evil" and "turn the other cheek" (5:39), as well as a version of the Golden Rule. Other lines often quoted are the references to "salt of the earth", "light of the world" and "judge not, lest ye be judged."

The reference to going up a mountain prior to preaching could be a deliberate reference to Moses on Mount Sinai, and many Christians believe that the Sermon on the Mount is actually a form of commentary on the Ten Commandments. However, we have no proof that this was the case. What we do know for a fact is that there are no mountains in the area where the sermon was delivered, but there are several large hills in the region to the west of the Sea of Galilee. For this reason, the Greek word used in Matthew 5:1 might better be translated as "mountainous region" or even "hills" rather than "mountain".

# Reference

Berman, M. (2010) *All God's Creatures: Stories Old and New*, California: Pendraig Publishing (for the story "The Child of God").

# 9
# Mount Ararat

Mount Ararat is a snow-capped, dormant volcanic cone in Turkey. It has two peaks: Greater Ararat (the tallest peak in Turkey, and the entire Armenian plateau with an elevation of 5,137 m/16,854 ft.) and Lesser Ararat (with an elevation of 3,896 m/12,782 ft.). The Ararat massif is about 40 km (25 mi) in diameter. The Iran-Turkey boundary skirts east of Lesser Ararat, the lower peak of the Ararat massif.

Mount Ararat in Judeo-Christian tradition is associated with the "Mountains of Ararat" where according to the book of Genesis, Noah's ark came to rest. The Bible does not refer to any specific mountain or peak, but rather a mountain range within the region of Ararat, which was the name of an ancient proto-Armenian kingdom also known as Urartu. In Armenian and European tradition, the mountain is believed to have been Mount Masis, the highest peak in the Armenian Highland, which is therefore called Mount Ararat. On the other hand, "the Semitic tradition associated this landing with the mountain called Judi Dagh (earlier called Ararad or Sararad) located in Kurdistan northeast of Mosul" (Hewsen, 2001, p.15).

According to the medieval Armenian historian Moses of Khoren in his *History of Armenia*, the plain of Ayrarat (directly north of the mountain) got its name after King Ara the Handsome (the great grandson of Amasya). Here the Assyrian Queen Semiramis is said to have lingered for a few days after the death of Ara. According to Thomson though, the mountain is called Ararat corresponding to Ayrarat, the name of the province.

It is not known when the last eruption of Ararat occurred; there are no historic or recent observations of large-scale activity recorded. It seems that Ararat was active in the 3rd millennium BC; under the pyroclastic flows, artifacts from the early Bronze Age and remains of human bodies have been found. However, it is known that Ararat was shaken by a large earthquake in July 1840, the effects of which were largest in the neighbourhood of the Ahora Gorge (a northeast trending chasm that drops 1,825 metres (5,988 ft.) from the top of the mountain). An unstable part of the northern slope collapsed and a chapel, a monastery, and a village were covered by rubble. According to some sources, Ararat erupted then as well, albeit under the ground water level.

Dr. Friedrich Parrot, with the help of Khachatur Abovian, was the first explorer in modern times to reach the summit of Mount Ararat, subsequent to the onset of Russian rule in 1829. Abovian and Parrot crossed the Aras River and headed to the Armenian village of Agori situated on the northern slope of Ararat 4,000 feet above sea level. Following the advice of Harutiun Alamdarian of Tbilisi, they set up a base camp at the Monastery of Saint Jacob some 2,400 feet higher, at an elevation of 6,375 feet. Abovian was one of the last travellers to visit Agori and the monastery before a disastrous earthquake completely buried both in May 1840. Their first attempt to climb the mountain, using the northeastern slope, failed as a result of lack of warm clothing.

Six days later, on the advice of Stepan Khojiants, the village chief of Agori, the ascent was attempted from the northwestern side. After reaching an elevation of 16,028 feet they turned back because they did not reach the summit before sundown. They reached the summit on their third attempt at 3:15 p.m. on October 9, 1829. Abovian dug a hole in the ice and erected a wooden cross facing north. Abovian also picked up a chunk of ice from the summit and carried it down with him in a bottle, considering the water holy.

Because of the political instability in Southeast Turkey, Ararat has been a militarized zone for much of the 20th century and was opened for tourism only in 2001. Since 2004, Ararat has been part of a nature reserve.

In Armenian mythology Mt. Ararat is the home of the Gods, much like Mt. Olympus is in Greek mythology, and it dominates the skyline of Armenia's capital, Yerevan. The mountain has been revered by the Armenians as symbolizing their national identity and their irredentism, featuring on their coat of arms and also depicted on various Armenian banknotes.

Mountains are not only living proof of the power of nature. They also act as a reminder to us that some summits can never be

reached. No bird can reach the mountain's crest and neither can any amount of wishing bring about the return of the warriors in this poem. There are some situations we just have to learn how to live with. And for a present-day Armenian, seeing Mount Ararat now situated across the border in Turkey every morning upon awakening, surely provides a prime example of this:

# NO BIRD CAN REACH THE MOUNTAIN'S CREST
# by Hovhannes Costaniantz

No bird can reach the mountain's crest.

There blow the winds that never rest;

And 'midst the stars that crown the height,

Saint Gregory's fair lamp shines bright. [1]

    Ah, gentle brother, sweet and brave,

    That Light thy sword and spirit save!

How many rills the mountain yields!

Those rills are streams, that dew the fields.

My brother sweet, those rushing streams

Are like my longings and my dreams.

    Happy the maid that loveth thee!

    When shall thy heart's desire be?

See, in the South a tempest breaks—

A tempest howls, the leaflet quakes;

---

1    Above the summit of Aragatz, the mountain that faces Ararat on the far side of the plain, a weird light is sometimes visible, traditionally called the Lamp of Saint Gregory the Illuminator
    The sense of longing for past glories and feelings of regret for what has been lost pervade the literature from Armenia, sentiments that are reflected in this poem about the mountain too:

The bluebell hangs its petals bright,

The cock cries out with all his might.

> Like showers of gold comes down the rain
>
> Why comes my love not home again?

The Star of Light begins his course,

The brave one mounts upon his horse.

He drives his spurs into its flanks,

And rides away to join the ranks.

> Happy the maid that loveth thee,
>
> When shall thy heart's desire be?

There comes no news from far away,

Our brave ones rest not from the fray.

'Tis long that sleep my eyes doth flee—

Our foemen press unceasingly.

> 'Tis long for sleep I vainly pray:
>
> There comes no news from far away.

# The Tears of Araxes
# by Raphael Patkanian

I WALK by Mother Arax
    With faltering steps and slow,
And memories of past ages
    Seek in the waters' flow.
But they run dark and turbid,
    And beat upon the shore
In grief and bitter sorrow,
    Lamenting evermore.

Araxes! with the fishes
    Why dost not dance in glee?
The sea is still far distant,
    Yet thou art sad, like me.
From thy proud eyes, O Mother,
    Why do the tears downpour?
Why dost thou haste so swiftly
    Past thy familiar shore?

Make not thy current turbid;
    Flow calm and joyously.
Thy youth is short, fair river;
    Thou soon wilt reach the sea.

Let sweet rose-hedges brighten

    Thy hospitable shore,

And nightingales among them

    Till morn their music pour.

Let ever-verdant willows

    Lave in thy waves their feet,

And with their bending branches

    Refresh the noonday heat.

Let shepherds on thy margin

    Walk singing, without fear;

Let lambs and kids seek freely

    Thy waters cool and clear."

Araxes swelled her current,

    Tossed high her foaming tide,

And in a voice of thunder

    Thus from her depths replied:—

Rash, thoughtless youth, why com'st thou

    My age-long sleep to break,

And memories of my myriad griefs

    Within my breast to wake?

When hast thou seen a widow,

    After her true-love died,

From head to foot resplendent

    With ornaments of pride?

For whom should I adorn me?

    Whose eyes shall I delight?

The stranger hordes that tread my banks

    Are hateful in my sight.

My kindred stream, impetuous Kur,

    Is widowed, like to me,

But bows beneath the tyrant's yoke,

    And wears it slavishly.

But I, who am Armenian,

    My own Armenians know;

I want no stranger bridegroom;

    A widowed stream I flow.

Once I, too, moved in splendour,

    Adorned as is a bride

With myriad precious jewels,

    My smiling banks beside.

My waves were pure and limpid,

    And curled in rippling play;

The morning star within them

    Was mirrored till the day.

What from that time remaineth?

    All, all has passed away.

Which of my prosperous cities

    Stands near my waves to-day?

Mount Ararat doth pour me,

    As with a mother's care,

From out her sacred bosom

    Pure water, cool and fair.

Shall I her holy bounty

    To hated aliens fling?

Shall strangers' fields be watered

    From good Saint Jacob's spring?

For filthy Turk or Persian

    Shall I my waters pour,

That they may heathen rites perform

    Upon my very shore,

While my own sons, defenceless,

    Are exiled from their home,

And, faint with thirst and hunger,

    In distant countries roam?

My own Armenian nation

    Is banished far away;

A godless, barbarous people

    Dwells on my banks to-day.

Shall I my hospitable shores

    Adorn in festive guise

For them, or gladden with fair looks

    Their wild and evil eyes?

Still, while my sons are exiled,

    Shall I be sad, as now.

This is my heart's deep utterance,

    My true and holy vow.

No more spake Mother Arax;

    She foamed up mightily,

And, coiling like a serpent,

    Wound sorrowing toward the sea.

        Translated by Alice Stone Blackwell.

Armenia is the smallest of the former Soviet republics, and is bounded by Georgia in the north, Azerbaijan in the east, Iran in the south, and Turkey in the west. Frequently referred to as one of the cradles of civilization, it is also considered by many to have been the first country in the world to officially embrace Christianity as its religion (c. 300). This is reflected in the folktales from the region, as can be seen in the story about climbing a mountain that follows:

# The Town of Stone

There was once an Armenian king, a ruler of a little town, who did not believe in God. "Who is God?" he would say to anyone who tried to change his mind.

No one was able to persuade the king, and because of his disbelief, the people of the town suffered. For ten years not one drop of rain fell, and vegetation of all kinds ceased to grow. The sheep could not find grass to graze and were dying. The people became hungry, and yet there was nothing they could do. They killed such animals as they had and ate them, but soon these, too, were all gone.

One day the people saw a strange thing happening among them. Many of them were slowly turning to stone, starting from their feet and moving upward. Soon all the people had become completely petrified. Then the king grew frightened that he, too, would turn to stone. "Guards," he ordered, "arrange everything so that the queen, myself and all my guards can climb that tall mountain and run away from this disease."

Very soon the king, the queen and all the king's guards, laden with food and tents, climbed the mountain in an attempt to get away from the disease. But do you think they could run away from God? No, they could not because God is everywhere.

Very soon the king began to turn to stone, starting from his feet. The queen was afflicted next and then the soldiers. In their foolishness they had imagined that they could hide from God, but not one of them was saved.

One day a traveller passing through the town saw that all the people had turned to stone. Surprised, he climbed the mountain near the town, and there he saw the king, the queen and all their guards standing as stones. He saw the beautiful crown which the queen had worn and decided to take it back home with him. But, as he lifted it off her head, it crumbled into dust. The man, seeing the danger that could come to him, left it there and ran as fast as he could down the mountain.

As far as we know, that town is still in existence, and the people in it are still petrified. And if a person should climb the mountain near the town, he would find the king, and the queen and all their guards, standing as quietly as stones (adapted from a tale told by Mrs. Mariam Serabian that was taken from Hoogasian-Villa, S., 1966, *100 Armenian Tales*, Detroit, Michigan: Wayne State University Press).

# References

*Armenian Legends and Poems* by Zabelle C. Boyajian. London: J. M. Dent & Sons Ltd. New York: Columbia University Press [1916]. NOTICE OF ATTRIBUTION. Scanned at sacred-texts.com, June 2006. Proofed and Formatted by John Bruno Hare. This text is in the public domain in the United States because it was published prior to January 1st, 1923. These files may be used for any non-commercial purpose, provided this notice of attribution is left intact in all copies.

Hewsen, Robert H. (2001), *Armenia: A Historical Atlas* (1st ed.), Chicago, IL: University of Chicago Press, ISBN 0-226-33228-4, http://www.press.uchicago.edu/Misc/Chicago/332284.html

Moses of Khoren; Thomson, Robert W. (1978). *History of the Armenians*. Cambridge, Massachusetts: Harvard University Press. ISBN 0-674-39571-9.

# 10
# Mount Koya-san, the Hermit's Cave, and Fujiyama

Almost all religions have some sacred mountains - either holy themselves (like Mount Olympus in Greek mythology, regarded as the home of the Greek Gods) or related to famous events (like Mount Sinai in Judaism and descendant religions). In some cases, though, the sacred mountain is purely mythical, like the Hara Berezaiti in Zoroastrianism. Volcanoes were also regarded as sacred mountains, such as Mount Etna in Italy, which was believed to be the home of Vulcan the Roman God of fire.

In Japan, Mount Koya-san is the home to one of the holiest Buddhist monastery complexes in the country. It was founded by a saint, Kukai, who is also known as Kobo Dashi and is regarded as a famous wandering mystic; his teachings are infamous throughout Japan and he is credited with being an important figure in shaping early Japanese culture. Buddhists believe that Kobo Dashi is not dead, but will instead awake and assist in bringing enlightenment to all people, alongside the Buddha and other bodhisattvas. It is believed that he was shown the sacred place to build the monastery by a forest god; this site is now the location of a large cemetery that is flanked by 120 esoteric Buddhist temples. Approximately a million pilgrims

The Old Hermit entertains the Children

Hanano San Takes the Cherry Branch From the Youth

visit Mount Koya-san a year; these pilgrims have included both royals and commoners who wish to pay their respects to Kobo Dashi. And the healing powers of saint Kukai, who founded the sacred temple on Mount Koya-san, are referred to in the traditional folktale that follows:

# The Hermit's Cave

MANY years ago there lived in the village of Nomugi, in Hida Province, an old farmer named Jinnai, with his wife. They had a daughter on whom they simply doted. Her name was Yuka. She was seven years of age, and an extremely beautiful child. Unfortunately, just at this age she developed something the matter with her leg, which grew worse and worse until the limb became deformed. O Yuka suffered no pain; but her parents were much troubled. Doctors, drugs, and the advice of many friends made Yuka's leg no better.

'How sad it will be for her later on!' thought her mother and father. 'Even now it is sad that she should have a deformed leg when she plays with other children.'

There being no help, Yuka and her parents had to make the best of things. In any case, Yuka was not the only deformity in the village. There were other cases.—One of Yuka's boy playmates, Tarako, had been born blind; and another, Rinkichi, was so deaf that he could hold his ear to the temple bell while the other children struck it, and he never heard the sound, though he felt a vibration. Well, these two were perhaps no better off than Yuka, and at last her parents began to console themselves. The child played about and seemed perfectly happy.

Nomugi village is at the foot of the great mountain

Norikuradake, which rises 10,500 feet, and is a wild place of volcanic origin.

Many of the children of Nomugi used to go daily and play on the grassy slope of an old dam at the end of the village. They would throw stones into the water, fish, sail boats, and pick flowers. The dam was a kind of club for the children. From morning to evening they were there, having with them their rice to eat.

One day, while thus playing, they were surprised by an old man with a long white beard approaching them. He came from the direction of the mountain. All stopped their games to watch him. He came on into their midst, and, patting them on the head, seemed to make friends naturally. Taking notice of Yuka's bad leg, the old man said: 'Come! How is this? Have not your parents tried to cure it?' Little Yuka answered that they had, but that they could not do any good. The old man made her lie down on the grass, and began to manipulate the leg, pulling it this way and that way, and rubbed in some red medicine which he took from a case. The old man then operated on Tarako the blind boy, and on Rinkichi the deaf one.

'Now, my children,' said he, 'you all love your fathers and mothers, and it will be a great pleasure to them to find you cured of your ailments. You are not well yet; but you will be, if you do what I tell you, in less than three or four days. You are not to mention having seen me until I tell you that you may—after you are cured. Tomorrow you will meet me at the flat rock under the cave on Mount Norikuradake. You know the place. Very well: until to-morrow good-bye, and if I find you do as I tell you I will make you all laugh by showing you some fancy tricks.' Then he trudged off in the direction whence he had come.

The children continued their play, thinking 'What a nice old

The Woodcutter saves the boy from the Robbers

man!' And, strange to say, O Yuka, as she walked home, felt her leg to be of greater use.

Very little attention is paid to Japanese children. They are nearly always good and well-behaved, little grown-up people in fact; and therefore they ate their suppers and went to bed as such, giving no account of their day's amusements, or of the strange old man.

Next day they went to the flat rock. As it was wet, they had not started until late; but they found the old man, and, though he had no time to play with them and show the tricks which he had promised, he attended to Yuka's leg, and to the dumb boy and the blind.

'Now go home,' he said, 'and come back here tomorrow. By the time you get home Yuka's leg will be well, Tarako will be able to see, and Rinkichi able to hear; and I am sure your relations will be delighted. To-morrow, if it is fine, you must come early, and we shall have lots of fun.'

Even before they got home everything came about as the old man had said. The three children were recovered. The villagers and the parents rejoiced together; but all were mystified as to who the magician could be.

'If he returns to the mountain, as the children say, then he must live in the cave,' said one. 'He must be a Sennin,' said another. 'It is rumoured that the most famous priest, Kukai shonin, who founded the sacred temple on Mount Koya-san, in Kii Province, was able to make these wondrous cures in children,' added another. But, with all the gossiping and conjectures, none could explain how it was possible to bring sight to a boy who had been born blind. At last someone suggested that two or three should follow the children secretly on the following day: by hiding themselves they might be able to see what happened. This excellent plan was adopted.

In the morning about thirty children started off at daybreak, followed, unknown to themselves, by two men of the village.

When the children arrived at the flat rock—which is said to be large enough to measure one thousand Japanese mats of six feet by three feet—they found the old man seated at one end of it. The two men who had followed hid themselves in some fine azalea bushes.

First they saw the old man rise to his feet, and then go over to the children and hear from the three cured ones how they felt, and how their parents had been pleased. Tarako was the most delighted, perhaps, of the three; for he had never seen the world before, or even his parents.

'Now, my children, you have come here to see me, and I am going to amuse you all. See here!' Saying this, the old man picked up some dead sticks, and, blowing at their ends, produced blossoming cherry branches, plum blossoms, and peach, and handed a branch of each to the girls. Next he took a stone and threw it into the air, and behold! it turned into a dove. Another turned into a hawk, or, in fact, into any bird a boy chose to name.

'Now,' said the old man, 'I will show you some animals that will make you laugh.' He recited some mystic verse, and monkeys came leaping on the flat rock and began to wrestle with one another. The children clapped their hands in delight; but one of the men who was hidden exclaimed in his astonishment:

'Who can this wizard be? No other but a wizard could do such things!'

The venerable old man heard, and, looking cautiously round, said:

'Children, I can do no more tricks to-day. My spell has gone. I will go to my home, and you had better go to yours. Farewell.'

So saying, the old man bowed to them, and turned up the mountain path, taking the direction of the cave.

The two men came out from their hiding, and they, with the children, tried to follow him. In spite of his great age, he was much more nimble than they among the rocks; but they got far enough to see him enter the cave. Some minutes later they came to the entrance, and bowed before it. The entrance was surrounded by fragrant flowers; but into its dark depths they did not venture.

Suddenly O Yuka pointed upwards, crying, 'There is the old grandfather!' They all looked up; and standing on a cloud was the old man, right over the summit of the mountain.

'Ah, now it is quite clear!' cried one of the men. 'It is the famous hermit of Mount Norikuradake.' They all bowed low, and then went home to report to the villagers what they had seen.

Subscriptions were collected; a small temple was built inside the cave, and they called it the 'Sendokutsu Temple,' which means The Sennin's Temple.

Taken from *Ancient Tales and Folklore of Japan* by Richard Gordon Smith. London, A. & C. Black [1918]. Scanned, proofed and formatted at sacred-texts.com, February 2006, by John Bruno Hare. This text is in the public domain in the United States because it was published prior to 1923.

The story is in effect a cautionary one, warning us that as soon as we attempt to use our logical-mathematical intelligence to analyse the miraculous powers of sacred sites or of saints, as the two men in hiding are clearly attempting to do, the magic can well be lost to us. For that is when the hermit departs from the scene.

Mount Fuji is another sacred mountain in Japan. Several Shinto temples flank its base, all to pay homage to the mountain. The common belief is that Fujiyama is the incarnation of the earth spirit itself. The Fuki-ko sect maintains that the mountain is a holy being, and the home to the goddess Sengen-sama. Annual fire festivals are held there in her honour. Fujiyama is also the site of pilgrimages, with reportedly 40,000 people climbing up to its summit every year.

# 11
# Sacred Towers

As well as mountains being regarded as sacred, there is also a history of towers being built and then being regarded as sacred places too – from our very own Glastonbury Tor to the Twin Towers destroyed by the terrorists of 9/11, from the Ivory Towers in which writers and artists find their inspiration to the biblical Tower of Babel.

The Glastonbury Tor is a hill at Glastonbury, Somerset, England, which features the roofless St. Michael's Tower. Tor is a local word of Celtic origin meaning 'rock outcropping' or 'hill'. The Tor has a striking location in the middle of a plain called the Summerland

**Glastonbury Tor**

Meadows, part of the Somerset Levels. The plain is actually reclaimed fenland out of which the Tor once rose like an island, but now, with the surrounding flats, is a peninsula washed on three sides by the River Brue. The remains of Glastonbury Lake Village nearby were identified in 1892, showing that there was an Iron Age settlement about 300–200 BC on what was an easily defended island in the fens. The spot seems to have been called Ynys yr Afalon (meaning "The Isle of Avalon") by the Britons, and it is believed by some to be the Avalon of Arthurian legend. The Tor has been associated with the name Avalon, and identified with King Arthur, since the alleged discovery of King Arthur and Queen Guinevere's neatly labelled coffins in 1191, recounted by Gerald of Wales. [cf. "The Exhumation of King Arthur at Glastonbury" Speculum, 9 (1934)].

With the 19th-century resurgence of interest in Celtic

**Brueghel-Tower of Babel**

mythology, the Tor became associated with Gwyn ap Nudd, who was first Lord of the Underworld, and later King of the Fairies, and the Tor came to be represented as an entrance to Annwn or Avalon, the land of the fairies.

A persistent myth of more modern origin is that of the Glastonbury Zodiac, an astrological zodiac of gargantuan proportions said to have been carved into the land along ancient hedgerows and trackways. The theory was first put forward in 1927 by Katherine Maltwood, an artist with an interest in the occult, who thought the zodiac was constructed approximately 5,000 years ago. However, the vast majority of the land said to be covered by the zodiac was under several feet of water at the proposed time of its construction.

It has also been suggested that Glastonbury Tor is one of the possible locations of the Holy Grail (see Hoddap, 2007). This is because it is close to the location of the monastery that housed the Nanteos Cup. Another speculation is that the Tor was reshaped into a spiral maze for use in religious ritual, incorporating the myth that the Tor was the location of the Underworld king's spiral castle.

As for the Tower of Babel, the story is found in Genesis 11:1-9, and appears in the King James Version as follows:

> 1 And the whole earth was of one language, and of one speech. 2 And it came to pass, as they journeyed from the east, that they found a plain in the land of Shinar; and they dwelt there. 3 And they said one to another, Go to, let us make brick, and burn them thoroughly. And they had brick for stone, and slime had they for mortar. 4 And they said, Go to, let us build us a city and a tower, whose top may reach unto heaven; and let us make us a name, lest we be scattered abroad upon the face of the whole earth. 5 And

the Lord came down to see the city and the tower, which the children built. 6 And the Lord said, Behold, the people is one, and they have all one language; and this they begin to do; and now nothing will be restrained from them, which they have imagined to do. 7 Go to, let us go down, and there confound their language, that they may not understand one another's speech. 8 So the Lord scattered them abroad from thence upon the face of all the earth: and they left off to build the city. 9 Therefore is the name of it called Babel; because the Lord did there confound the language of all the earth: and from thence did the Lord scatter them abroad upon the face of all the earth.

The narrative of the Tower of Babel (Genesis 11:1-9) is an etiology, a narrative that explains the origin of a custom, ritual, geographical feature, name, or other phenomenon. The story of the Tower of Babel explains the origins of the multiplicity of languages. Yahweh was concerned that humans had too much freedom to do as they wished, so as punishment Yahweh brought into existence multiple languages. Thus, humans were divided into linguistic groups, and unable to understand each other, as they had previously been able to. A parallel can be drawn between this, and the way in which man is said to have once been able to understand the language of the animals and communicate with them, for this ability has been lost by us too.

The Tower of Babel has often been associated with known structures, notably the Etemenanki (Sumerian: "temple of the foundation of heaven and earth"), a ziggurat dedicated to Marduk by Nabopolassar (c. 610 BC). The Great Ziggurat of Babylon base was square (not round), 91 metres (300 ft) in height, but demolished by Alexander the Great before his death in an attempt to rebuild it. A Sumerian story with some similar elements is preserved in *Enmerkar and the Lord of Aratta* and the biblical story of the Tower of Babel could well have been influenced by Etemenanki during the Babylonian captivity of the Hebrews. Only the base of the ziggurat now remains, visible from Google Earth, which places its location at 32.5362583N and 44.4208252E just south of Baghdad.

Rabbinic literature offers many different accounts of other causes for building the Tower of Babel, and of the intentions of its builders. The Mishnah (the first written record of the Jewish Oral Law, c AD 200) describes the Tower as a rebellion against God. Some later midrash record that the builders of the Tower, called "the generation of secession" in the Jewish sources, said: "God has no right to choose the upper world for Himself, and to leave the lower world to us; therefore we will build us a tower, with an idol on the top holding a sword, so that it may appear as if it intended to war with God" (Gen. R. xxxviii. 7; Tan., ed. Buber, Noah, xxvii. et seq.).

The building of the Tower was meant to bid defiance not only to God, but also to Abraham, who exhorted the builders to reverence. The passage mentions that the builders spoke sharp words against God, not cited in the Bible, saying that once every 1,656 years, heaven tottered so that the water poured down upon the earth, therefore they would support it by columns that there might not be another deluge (Gen. R. l.c.; Tan. l.c.; similarly Josephus, "Ant." i. 4, § 2).

Some among that sinful generation even wanted to war against God in heaven (Talmud Sanhedrin 109a.) They were encouraged in this wild undertaking by the notion that arrows which they shot into the sky fell back dripping with blood, so that the people really believed that they could wage war against the inhabitants of the heavens (Sefer ha-Yashar, Noah, ed. Leghorn, 12b).

Though not mentioned by name, the Qur'an has a story with similarities to the biblical story of the Tower of Babel, though set in the Egypt of Moses. In Suras 28:38 and 40:36-37, Pharaoh asks Haman to build him a stone, or clay tower so that he can mount up to heaven and confront the God of Moses.

Another story in Sura 2:102 mentions the name of Babil, but tells of when the two angels Haroot and Maroot taught the people of Babylon the tricks of magic and warned them that magic is a sin and that their teaching them magic is a test of faith. A tale about Babil appears more fully in the writings of Yaqut (i, 448 f.) and the Lisan el-'Arab (xiii. 72), but without the tower: mankind were swept together by winds into the plain that was afterward called "Babil", where they were assigned their separate languages by God, and were then scattered again in the same way.

In the History of the Prophets and Kings by the 9th century Muslim theologian al-Tabari, a fuller version is given: Nimrod, the grandson of Ham (the son of Noah), has the tower built in Babil, God destroys it, and the language of mankind, formerly Syriac, is then confused into 72 languages. Another Muslim historian of the 13th century, Abu al-Fida relates the same story, adding that the patriarch Eber (an ancestor of Abraham) was allowed to keep the original tongue, Hebrew in this case, because he would not partake in the building.

One theory, first advanced by David Rohl, associates Nimrod, the hunter, builder of Erech and Babel, with Enmerkar (i.e., Enmer the Hunter) king of Uruk, also said to have been the first builder of the Eridu temple. This theory proposes that the remains of the historical building that via Mesopotamian legend inspired the story of the Tower of Babel are the ruins of the ziggurat of Eridu, just south of Ur. Among the reasons for this association are the larger size of the ruins, the older age of the ruins, and the fact that one title of Eridu was NUN.KI ("mighty place"), which later became a title of Babylon. Both cities also had temples called the E-Sagila.

Various traditions similar to that of the Tower of Babel are also found in Central America. One holds that Xelhua, one of the seven giants rescued from the deluge, built the Great Pyramid of Cholula in order to storm heaven. The Gods destroyed it with fire and confounded the language of the builders. The Dominican friar Diego Duran (1537–1588) reported hearing this account from a hundred-year-old priest at Cholula, shortly after the conquest of Mexico.

Another story, attributed by the native historian Don Ferdinand d'Alva Ixtilxochitl (c. 1565-1648) to the ancient Toltecs, states that after men had multiplied following a great deluge, they erected a tall zacuali or tower, to preserve themselves in the event of a second deluge. However, their languages were confounded and they went to separate parts of the earth.

Still another story, attributed to the Tohono O'odham Indians, holds that Montezuma escaped a great flood, then became wicked and attempted to build a house reaching to heaven, but the Great Spirit destroyed it with thunderbolts. (Bancroft, vol. 3, p. 76).

The symbol of the tower has been appropriated by other religious groups too. For example, Watchtower is both the name of the official Web Site of the Jehovah's Witnesses and the name of the free magazine their adherents distribute.

There is also the idiom "a tower of strength" to refer to someone who can be relied on to provide support and comfort. As for its origin, it derives from The Book of Common Prayer, 1549: "O lorde... Bee unto them a tower of strength." And Shakespeare later used it in Richard III, 1594: "The king's name is a tower of strength."

Additionally, the tower features in Reiki, where it is known as a Healing Tower. The practice of tower healing involves a group effort with healers concentrating beams of Reiki energies on a specific area on a person's body that needs focused attention. Healers will stack the palms of their hands upon one another forming a healing tower, and this is commonly used as a tool during Reiki Shares.

Mention should also be made of Watch Towers, originally from the Enochian branch of Ceremonial Magick, and now incorporated into other traditions of Wicca. These are the four elemental "directions" or "quarters" (corresponding to the appropriate points on the compass) called to protect the Circle during its establishment. Each of them has a correspondence between the compass point, an element, and (varying amongst different traditions) a colour.

Another use of the tower is as the sixteenth trump or Major Arcana card in most cartomancy Tarot decks. To some, it symbolizes failure, ruin and catastrophe. To others, the Tower represents the paradigms constructed by the ego, the sum total of all schema that the mind constructs to understand the universe. The Tower is struck by lightning when reality does not conform to expectation.

The drawing of the card suggests the querent may be holding on to false ideas or pretences, and a new approach to the problem is needed. Others believe that the Tower represents dualism, and the smashing of dualism into its component parts, in preparation for renewal that does not come from reified, entrenched concepts. In other words, a new way of seeing things is called for.

Last but not least, there is The Tower of Wisdom, found

Tarot card from the Rider-Waite tarot deck

frequently in diagram collections of the thirteenth and fourteenth centuries. It was part of a tradition of architectural mnemonic aids going back to the "memory palaces" promoted by the Roman author Cicero. It also served as an object of meditation and a path to spiritual growth; by internalizing its principles, a patient student (often a monk) pursued the path of moral rectitude. Although each example is different, they all feature four columns, four windows, and a set of stairs. The four base columns denote what are known as the four cardinal virtues: Prudence, Fortitude, Justice, and Temperance.

\* \* \*

To return now to the starting point of this chapter, the Tower of Babel, there are numerous accounts of why the Tower was built and also to explain the reason for its destruction. My own interpretation, however, would be this: it was built as a result of man's irrepressible desire to show he / she is in control of his own destiny despite the fact that this is clearly not the case, as is shown by all the natural disasters that occur to dent man's confidence in such a belief. As to why it was destroyed, whenever we attempt to analyse away the magic of our, or of others', creativity, we ultimately end up destroying it because the magic is dependent on our left brain appreciation of it.

The right brain of the brain focuses on the visual, and processes information in an intuitive and simultaneous way, looking first at the whole picture then the details. The focus of the left brain, on the other hand, is verbal – processing information in an analytical and sequential way, looking first at the pieces then putting them together to get the whole. Our education system tends to discourage right brain thinking and the construction, as well as the destruction, of the Towers of Babel we build can be seen to be the inevitable result of this.

## References

Bancroft, H.H. (1874) *Native Races of the Pacific States.* New York: Appleton.

Hoddap, C., & Von Kannon, A. (2007) *The Templar Code for Dummies.* Hoboken, NJ: Wiley Publishing Inc.

Hutton, R. (2003) *Witches, Druids and King Arthur.* Hammersmith, London: Continuum Books.

Mann, N.R. (1993) *Glastonbury Tor: A guide to the history and legends.* Butleigh, Somerset: Triskele publications.

Rahtz, P. (1993) *Glastonbury.* English Heritage/Batsford.

Rohl, D. (1998) *Legend: The Genesis of Civilization.* London: Century.

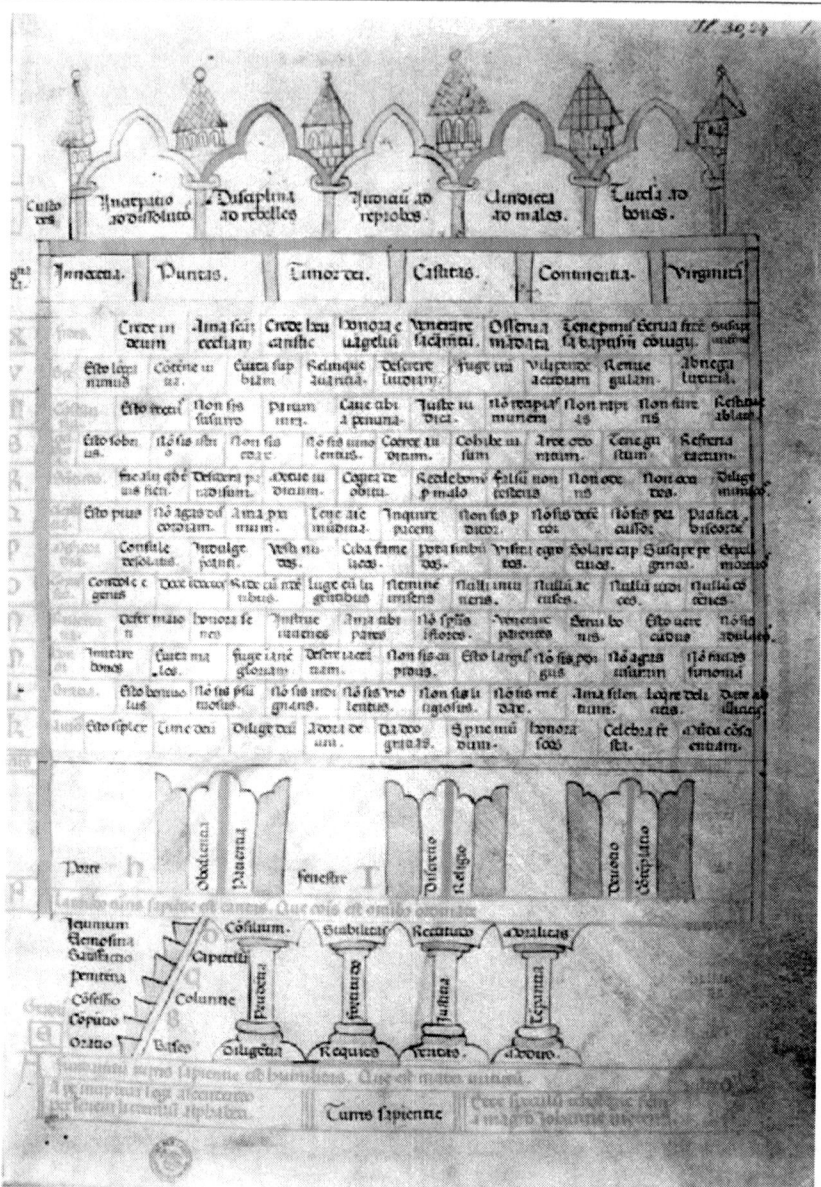

Tower of Wisdom

# 12

# The Fool on the Hill and the Book of Mysteries

**The fool on the hill
Sees the sun going down,
And the eyes in his head,
See the world spinning 'round.**

The Beatles sang of *The Fool on the Hill* – the man who chose to go within and learn from his Inner Teacher there. Others have gone into the hills or the mountains to find wisdom too, and this chapter focuses on perhaps one of the generally less known ones, at least outside the Jewish tradition, namely the Baal Shem Tov.

Two hundred years ago, in a remote hut in the Carpathian Mountains, there lived a wonder-worker named Rabbi Israel. Some now say that he never existed; the like has been said of King Arthur and of Jesus Christ; their legends remain with us, and so does his.

Although he knew all the secret mysteries of Cabbala, he refused to lead the stifled life of the synagogue scholar, turned his back upon what he considered to be pointless splitting of hairs that the rabbis would engage in over minutae of the law, and withdrew to the mountains, where he would wander alone, sometimes for many days at a time, absorbed in his strange reflections.

And when Israel eventually came down from the mountains, it was to teach men to live with abounding joy. For joy in every living thing, he said, is the very highest form of worship. The woods were holy, and the fields, every stone and blade of grass contained a spark of the living Soul; every act of living: breathing, eating, walking should be accomplished with fervour, joy, ecstasy, for every act spoke to God.

He did not violate tradition through such teachings, though; in fact, he did just the opposite – he enlarged it. He was observant of every point of the law, and he revered the house of prayer; but he said that divinely simple truth that becomes lost in the ritual of every religion. The full-hearted desire to worship was more important than the form or place of worship, as far as he was concerned, and that is what he believed in and taught. What follows is one of the legends told about him, taken from *The Golden Mountain: Marvellous Tales of Rabbi Israel Baal Shem and of his Great-grandson, Rabbi Nachmann* retold from Hebrew, Yiddish and German sources by Meyer Levin. Illustrated by Marek Szwarc. New York: Behrman House Inc. Publishers [1932]. The book is in the public domain and can be found on the Sacred Texts website: www.sacred-texts.com The story is set in the town of Okup, where Rabbi Israel was born, and where he later returned to become the watcher of the synagogue there.

# The Book of Mysteries

IN THIS STORY WE LEARN HOW THE BAAL SHEM TOV RECEIVED THE BOOK OF ADAM, AND OF THE FRIGHTFUL END THAT CAME TO THE SON OF RABBI ADAM

... The desire for knowledge came into him; and the joy that was given him by flowers and beasts in the forest was no longer sufficient. His mind was afire and thirsty, but his thirst could be quenched only by those waters that had cooled for ages deep in the deepest wells of mystery, and the fire within him was of the sort that burns forever, and does not consume.

The innermost secrets of the Cabbala were for him, and they were only as stars of night against the sun. For to him would be revealed the Secret of Secrets.

The boy lived in the synagogue. But since the time for the revelation of his power was yet far away, he did not show his passion for the Torah to the men of the synagogue. By day, he slept on the benches, pretending to be a clod. But as soon as the last of the scholars blew out his candle and crept on his way toward home, Israel rose, and took the candle into a corner, and lighted it, and all night long he stood and read the Torah.

In another city the Tzaddik Rabbi Adam, master of all mysteries, waited the coming of his last day. For in each generation one is chosen to carry throughout his lifetime the candle that is lighted from heaven. And the candle may never be set down. And the soul of the Tzaddik may not return to eternal peace in the regions above until another such soul illuminates the earth.

Rabbi Adam was even greater than the Tzaddikim who had been before him. For in the possession of Rabbi Adam was the Book that contains the Word of eternal might.

Though Rabbi Adam was not one of the Innocent souls, he had led a life so pure that this Book had been given into his hands. Before him, only six human beings had possessed the knowledge that was in the Book of Adam. The Book was given to the first man, Adam, and it was given to Abraham, to Joseph, to Joshua ben Nun, and to Solomon. And the seventh to whom it was given was the Tzaddik, Rabbi Adam.

This is how he came to receive the Book.

When he had learned all Torah, and all Cabbala, he had not been content, but had searched day and night for the innermost secret of power. When he knew all the learning that there was among men, he said, "Man does not know." And he had begged of the angels.

One night Rabbi Adam arose from his sleep. He walked into a wilderness. Before him stood a mountain, and in the side of the mountain was a cave. And that was one mouth of the cave, whose other mouth was in the Holy Land. It was the cave of the Machpelah, where Abraham lies buried.

Rabbi Adam went deep into the cave, and there he found the Book.

All of his life Rabbi Adam has guarded the secret of knowledge. Gazing into it, he had grown old, and he had come to see with the grave eyes of one who sees to the end of things.

And when he saw himself growing old, he began to ask, "What will become of my wisdom?"

Then he rose, and looked to the Lord and said, "To whom, Almighty God, shall I leave the Book of Wisdom? Give me a son, that I may teach him."

He was given a son. His son grew, and became learned in the Torah. The Rabbi taught his son all that there was in the Torah. And he said, "My son learns well." He began to teach his son the Cabbala. His son was sharp in understanding. But when the boy had learned the secrets of the Cabbala, he asked no more. Then the old heart of Rabbi Adam was weary and yearned for death. "My son is not the one," he said.

Night after night Rabbi Adam prayed to the Almighty that he might be relieved of the burden of knowledge. And one night the word came to him, saying, "Give the Book into the hands of Rabbi

Israel, son of Eleazer, who lives in Okup."

Rabbi Adam was thankful, for now he might give over his burden, and die. He said to his son, "Here is one book in which I have not read with you."

His son asked, "Was I not worthy?"

"You are not the predestined vessel," said Rabbi Adam. "You would break with the heat of the fluid."

Then he said to his son, "Seek out Rabbi Israel, in the city of Okup, for these leaves belong to him. And if he will be favourable toward you and receive you as his servant and instruct you in his Torah, then count yourself happy. For, my son, you must know that it is your fate to be the squire who gives into the hands of his knight the sword that has been tempered and sharpened by hundreds of divine spirits that now lie silent under the earth."

Soon Rabbi Adam died. His son did not think of himself, but thought only of fulfilling the mission his father had given into his charge. He deserted the city of his birth and, taking with him the leaves of the Book, went in search of that Rabbi Israel of whom his father had spoken.

The son of Rabbi Adam came to the town of Okup. He wished to keep secret the true reason of his coming, so he said, "I am seeking a bride. I would marry, and live my life here." The people of the town were delighted, and felt greatly honoured because the son of the Tzaddik, Rabbi Adam, had chosen to live among them.

Every day he went to the synagogue. There he encountered scholars, and holy men, and rabbis. He asked their names of them. But he did not meet with any one called Rabbi Israel, son of Rabbi Eleazer.

Often, when all the others had gone from the synagogue, Rabbi

Adam's son remained studying the Torah. Then he noticed that the boy who served in the synagogue also remained there, he saw that the eyes of the boy were bright with inner knowledge, and that his face was strained with unworldly happiness.

Rabbi Adam's son went to the elders of the house of prayer and said to them, "Let me have a separate room in which to study. Perhaps I shall want to sleep there sometimes when I study late into the night. Then give me the boy Israel as a servant."

"Why has he chosen the boy Israel, who is a clod?" the elders asked.

Then they remembered that Israel was the son of Rabbi Eleazer. "He has chosen him to honour the memory of his father, Eleazer, who was a very holy man," they said.

When the boy came to serve him, the son of Rabbi Adam asked, "What is your name?"

"Israel, son of Eleazer."

The master watched the boy, and soon came to feel certain that this was indeed the Rabbi Israel whom he sought.

One night he remained late in the synagogue. He lay down on a bench, and pretended to be asleep. He opened his eyes a little, and he saw how the boy Israel arose and took a candle and lighted it, and covered the light, standing in a corner and studying the Torah. For many hours the boy remained motionless in an intensity of study that the rabbi had known only in his father, the Tzaddik Rabbi Adam.

All night long the boy studied. And when the sunrise embraced his candle flame, he slipped down upon the bench, and slept.

Then the rabbi arose and took a leaf from the holy book his father had given him, and placed the leaf on the breast of Israel.

Soon the boy stirred, and sleeping reached his hand toward the page of writing. He held the page before his eyes, and opened his eyes and read. As he read, he rose. He bent over the page of mysteries, and studied it, and his whole face was aflame, his eyes glowed as if they had pierced into the heart of the earth, and his hands burned as if they lay against the heart of the earth.

When full day came, the boy fell powerless upon the bench, and slept.

The rabbi sat by him and watched over him until he awoke again. Then the rabbi placed his hand upon the boy's hand that held the leaf out of the book. The rabbi took the other pages of the book, and gave them to him, saying: "Know, that I place in your hands the infinite wisdom that God gave forth on Mount Sinai. The words that are in this book have been entrusted only in the hearts of the chosen of the chosen, when no soul on earth was worthy to contain its wisdom, this book lay hidden from man. For centuries it was buried in unreachable depths. But always there came the time for its uncovering, again it was brought to light, again lost. My father was the last of the great souls to whom it was entrusted. I was not found worthy of retaining it, and through my hands my father transmits this book to your hands. I beg of you, Rabbi Israel, allow me to be your servant, let me be as the air about you, absorbing your holy words, that otherwise would be lost in nothingness."

Israel answered, "Let it be so. We will go out of the city, and give ourselves over to the study of this book."

The son of Rabbi Adam went with Israel to live in a house that stood outside of the town. There, day and night, they were absorbed in the study of the pages that contained the words of all the mysteries.

Israel was as one who feeds on honey and walks on golden clouds. His soul swelled with tranquil joy, and his heart was filled with the peace of understanding. Often, he went with the leaves of the book into the forest, and there, the words of the book were as the words spoken to him by the flowers and by the beasts.

But the son of Rabbi Adam was eaten by that upon which he fed, and yet his hunger grew ever more insatiable. The grander the visions that opened before him, the greater was the cavern within himself. And he was afraid, as one who stands on a great height and looks downward.

Each day, his eyes sank deeper, and became more red.

Rabbi Israel, seeing the illness that was come into his companion, said to him, "What is it that consumes you? What is it that you desire?"

Then the son of Rabbi Adam said, "Only one thing can give me rest. All that has been revealed to me has set me flaming with a single curiosity, and each new mystery that is solved before me only causes a greater chaos in my mind, and a greater hunger in my heart."

"What is the one thing that you desire?"

"Reveal the Word to me!"

"The Word is inviolate!" cried Rabbi Israel.

But the son of Rabbi Adam fell on his knees and cried, "Until I see the end of all wisdom, I cannot come to rest! Call down the highest of powers, the Giver of the Torah Himself, force Him to come down to us, otherwise I am lost!"

Then the Master shrank from him. He said, "The hour has not yet come for His descent to earth."

His companion was silent. He never pleaded with Israel again.

But each day Rabbi Israel saw his face become darker, and his body become more feeble. The hands were weak, and could hardly turn a leaf.

Rabbi Israel was torn with pity for his companion.

At last he said, "Is it still your wish that we name the Giver of the Torah, and call Him to earth once more?"

The son of Rabbi Adam remained silent. But he lifted his eyes to the eyes of Rabbi Israel. They were as the eyes of the dead come to life.

"Then we must purify our souls, that they may reach the uttermost power of will."

On Friday, the two rabbis went to the mikweh, where they bathed in the spring of holy water. From Sabbath to Sabbath they fasted, and when they reached the height of their fast they went again to the mikweh, and purified themselves in the bath.

On the second Friday night they stood in their house of prayer. They called upon their own souls and said, "Are you pure?" Their souls answered, "We have been purified."

Then Rabbi Israel raised his hands into the darkness, and cried out the terrible Name.

The son of Rabbi Adam raised his arms aloft, and his feeble lips moved as he repeated the unknowable Word.

But in the instant that the word left those lips, Israel touched him and said, "My brother, you have made an error! Your command was wrongly uttered, it has been caught by the wind, it has been carried to the Lord of Fire! We are in the hands of death."

"I am lost," said the son of Rabbi Adam, "for I am not pure."

"Only one way is left to us," cried Rabbi Israel. "We must watch until day comes. If one of us closes an eyelid, the evil one will seize him, he is lost."

Then they began to watch. They stood guard over their souls. With their eyes open they watched. And the hours passed. They stood in prayer, and the hours passed.

But as dawn came, the son of Rabbi Adam, enfeebled by his week of purification, and by the long struggle against the darkness of night, wavered, his head nodded, and sank upon the table.

Rabbi Israel reached out his arm to raise him. But in that moment an unseen thing sped from the mouth of Rabbi Adam's son, and a flame devoured his heart, and his body sank to the ground.

**The Book of Mysteries**

**Mount Kanla-on**

**Kanlaon-Volcano**

# 13

# The Tobacco of Harisaboqued

For those misguided souls who fail to respect, or take for granted, all that is sacred, who believe they can control the Great Mystery we are part of, who have the arrogance to suppose they can eradicate all illness or find the secret to everlasting life, gain nothing but disappointment lies in wait, as the following folktale from the Philippines, serves to illustrate.

The mountain of Canlaon is named after Kan-Laon, an ancient Visayan deity. During pre-Hispanic times, the deity was worshiped by the natives as their Supreme Ruler. Kan-Laon means "One Who Is the Ruler Of Time".

The mountain, situated on the island of Negros, is the largest active volcano in the Philippines and highest mountain in the Visayas region. It is said to be where Laon made his presence known to the people. In ancient times, native priests (babaylan) would climb up the mountain and do rituals every good harvest season or when there was a special ceremony to be performed. They would also offer gifts as a sign of respect.

\* \* \*

A legend of the volcano of Canlaon on the island of Negros. It is told generally in Western Negros and Eastern Cebu. The volcano is still active, and smoke and steam rise from its crater.

Long before the strange men came over the water from Spain, there lived in Negros, on the mountain of Canlaon, an old man who had great power over all the things in the earth. He was called Harisaboqued, King of the Mountain.

When he wished anything done he had but to tap the ground three times and instantly a number of little men would spring from the earth to answer his call. They would obey his slightest wish, but as he was a kind old man and never told his dwarfs to do anything wrong, the people who lived near were not afraid. They planted tobacco on the mountain side and were happy and prosperous.

The fields stretched almost to the top of the mountain and the plants grew well, for every night Harisaboqued would order his dwarfs to attend to them, and though the tobacco was high up it grew faster and better than that planted in the valley below.

The people were very grateful to the old man and were willing to do anything for him; but he only asked them not to plant above a line he had ordered his little men to draw around the mountain near the top. He wished that place for himself and his dwarfs.

All obeyed his wish and no one planted over the line. It was a pretty sight to see the long rows of tobacco plants extending from the towns below far up to the line on the mountain side.

One day Harisaboqued called the people together and told them that he was going away for a long time. He asked them again not to plant over the line, and told them that if they disregarded this wish he would carry all the tobacco away and permit no more to grow on the mountain side until he had smoked what he had taken. The people promised faithfully to obey him. Then he tapped on the ground, the earth opened, and he disappeared into the mountain.

Many years passed and Harisaboqued did not come back. All

wondered why he did not return and at last decided that he would never do so. The whole mountain side was covered with tobacco and many of the people looked with greedy eyes at the bare ground above the line, but as yet they were afraid to break their promise.

At last one man planted in the forbidden ground, and, as nothing happened, others did the same, until soon the mountain was entirely covered with the waving plants. The people were very happy and soon forgot about Harisaboqued and their promise to him.

But one day, while they were laughing and singing, the earth suddenly opened and Harisaboqued sprang out before them. They were very much frightened and fled in terror down the mountain side. When they reached the foot and looked back they saw a terrible sight. All the tobacco had disappeared and, instead of the thousands of plants that they had tended so carefully, nothing but the bare mountain could be seen.

Then suddenly there was a fearful noise and the whole mountain top flew high in the air, leaving an immense hole from which poured fire and smoke.

The people fled and did not stop until they were far away. Harisaboqued had kept his word.

Many years have come and gone, but the mountain is bare and the smoke still rolls out of the mountain top. Villages have sprung up along the sides, but no tobacco is grown on the mountain. The people remember the tales of the former great crops and turn longing eyes to the heights above them, but they will have to wait. Harisaboqued is still smoking his tobacco.

Taken from *Philippine Folklore Stories* by John Maurice Miller, Boston: Ginn. [1904]. This text is in the public domain in the US because it was published prior to January 1st, 1923.

# 14

# The Princess of the Tower

For some of us, only by leaving this world behind and going within can we find the treasure hard to attain, and to do this we need to climb the loftiest of peaks or towers. However, even that is not enough though, for then comes the time for reincorporation – to return to this reality with what we have learnt so that others may benefit from it – and that is what this final tale deals with.

### I.

Princess Solima was sick, not exactly ill, but so much out of sorts that her father, King Zuliman, was both annoyed and perturbed. The princess was as beautiful as a princess of those days should be; her long tresses were like threads of gold, her blue eyes rivaled the color of the sky on the balmiest summer day; and her smile was as radiant as the sunshine itself.

She was learned and clever, too, and her goodness of heart gained for her as great a renown as her peerless beauty. Despite all this, Princess Solima was not happy. Indeed, she was wretched to despondency, and her melancholy weighed heavily upon her father.

"What ails you, my precious daughter?" he asked her a hundred times, but she made no answer.

She just sat and silently moped. She did not waste away, which puzzled the physicians; she did not grow pale, which surprised her attendants; and she did not weep, which astonished herself. But she

**The Princess of the Tower**

felt as if her heart had grown heavy, as if there was no use in anything.

The king squared his shoulders to show his determination and summoned his magicians and wizards and sorcerers and commanded them to perform their arts and solve the mystery of the illness of Princess Solima. A strange crew they were, ranged in a semi-circle before the king. There was the renowned astrologer from Egypt, a little man with a humpback; the mixer of mysterious potions from China, a long, lank yellow man, with tiny eyes; the alchemist from Arabia, a scowling man with his face almost concealed by whiskers; there was a Greek and a Persian and a Phoenician, each with some special knowledge and fearfully anxious to display it. They set to work.

One studied the stars, another concocted a sweet-smelling fluid, a third retired to the woods and thought deeply, a fourth made abstruse calculations with diagrams and figures, a fifth questioned the princess' handmaidens, and a sixth conceived the brilliant notion of talking with the princess herself. He was certainly an original wizard, and he learned more than all the others.

Then they met in consultation and talked foreign languages and pretended very seriously to understand one another. One said the stars were in opposition, another said he had gazed into a crystal and had seen a glow-worm chasing a hippopotamus which a third interpreted as meaning the princess would die if the glow-worm won the race.

"Rubbish!" exclaimed the magician who had spoken to the princess; "likewise stuff and nonsense and the equivalent thereof in the seventy unknown languages."

That was an impertinent comment on their divinations, and so they listened seriously.

"The princess," he said, "is just tired. That is a disease which will become popular and fashionable as the world grows older and more people amass riches. She is sick of being waited on hand and foot and bowed down to and all that sort of thing. She has never been allowed to romp as a child, to choose her own companions and the rest of it. Therefore, she is bored with all the etceteras. The case is comprehensible and comprehensive: it needs the exercise of imagination stimulated by prescience, conscience, patience . . . ."

The others yawned and began to collect dictionaries, and fearing that they might be tempted to fling them at him after they had found the meaning of his big words, he ceased.

"I agree," said the president of the assembly, the oldest wizard, "only I diagnose the disease in simpler form. The princess is in love."

That set them all jabbering together, and they finally agreed to report to the king that the time had arrived when the princess should marry, so that she should be able to go away to a new land, amid other people and different scenes.

The king agreed reluctantly, for he dearly loved his daughter and wished her to remain with him always if possible. Heralds and messengers were sent out far and wide, and very soon a procession of suitors for the princess' hand began to file past the lady. They were princes of all shapes and sizes, of all complexions and colors; some were resplendent with jewels, others were followed by retinues of slaves bearing gifts; a few entered the competition by proxy— that is, they sent somebody else to see the lady first and pronounce judgment upon her. These she dismissed summarily, declaring that they were disqualified by the rules of fair play.

When all the entrants had been inspected by the king, he said to his daughter: "Pick the one you love the best, Solima dear."

"None," she answered promptly.

"Dear, dear me—that is very awkward. We shall have to return the entrance fees—I mean the presents," he said.

That prospect did not seem to worry the princess in the least; nor did her father's appeal not to belittle him in the eyes of his fellow monarchs have the slightest effect on her.

"At least," he said, growing impatient, "tell me what you do want."

"I will marry any man," she replied, while he wondered gravely what else she could have said, "who is not such a fool as to think himself the only person in the world who is of consequence."

The king was not without wisdom, and he knew that this remark is foolish, or sensible, according to the mood in which it is said, and the thoughts behind it.

"You do not regard any one of the princes," the king said gently, "as worthy of ———"

"Any woman," interrupted his daughter. "Listen, my father, you have tried to make me happy always and until recently you have succeeded. I wish to obey you in all things, even in the choice of a husband. Would you really have me marry any one of these fools? Be not angry. Did any one reveal a gleam of wisdom, or common-sense? Were they not all just ridiculous fops? Let me enumerate:

There was Prince Hafiz who talked only of his wars—of the men—aye and women and children—his soldiers had butchered. The soldiers fought and Prince Hafiz posed before me as a warrior and hero. I will not be queen in a land where people cannot live in peace.

Then there was Prince Aziz who boasted that he spends all his life with his horses and dogs and falcons in the hunting field. He knows the needs of beasts, but not of men. I will not be the bride of a prince who allows his subjects to starve in wretchedness and poverty while he enjoys himself with the slaughter of wild beasts.

Prince Guzman had nothing else to impart to me but his taste in jewels and dress. Prince Abdul knew exactly how many bottles of wine he drank daily, but he could not tell me how many schools there were in his city. Prince Hassan had not the slightest notion how the majority of his people lived, whether by trading, or thieving, or working, or begging."

King Zuliman listened intently. This was a singular speech for a princess, but reason told him this was profoundest wisdom.

"Oh, I am tired," burst out Princess Solima, in tears. "I have no desire for life if to be a ruler over men and women and children means that you must take no interest in their welfare. My father, hearken. I will not be queen in a land where the king thinks the people live only to make him great. I shall be proud and happy to reign where the king understands that it is his duty to make his people happy and his country prosperous and peaceful."

The king left his daughter, and, deeply concerned, sought his wizards.

"My daughter has been born thousands of years before her time," he declared, petulantly. "The stars have played a trick on me, and have sent me my great-great-great-great ever so much great granddaughter out of her turn."

The magicians did not laugh at this: they thought it a wonderfully sage remark, and after much mysterious whispering among themselves and consultation of old books, and gazing into crystals, they informed the king that the stars foretold that Princess Solima would marry a poor man!

They flattered themselves on their cleverness in arriving at this conclusion, which they deduced from the princess' contempt for princes.

King Zuliman's patience was exhausted by this time. In a towering rage, he told his daughter what the wizards had said, and when she merely said, "How nice," he swore he would imprison her in his fortress in the sea.

His majesty meant it, too, and at once had the fortress, which stood on a tiny island miles from land, luxuriously furnished and fitted up for his daughter's reception. Thither she was conveyed secretly one night, but to her father's disgust she made no protest.

"I shall be free for a while," she said, "of all the absurd flummery of the palace."

## II.

The people were sad when the princess disappeared. She had been good and kind to them, had understood them, and they did not know whether she had died, or had deserted them without a word of farewell, though that was hardly possible. All that they knew was that the king suddenly became morose and sullen. Strangely enough, he began to take an interest in the poor. He asked them funny questions—for a king. How did they earn money? What was their occupation? Had they any pleasures? And what were their thoughts?

Young people laughed, but old men said the king intended to promote laws which would do good. Anyway, the king's interest did make his subjects happier, and the officers of state became very busy with projects and schemes for improving trade, providing work and for educating children.

"They do say," remarked one old woman, who kept an apple stall in the market place, "that a law will be passed that the sun should shine every day, and that it should never rain on the days of the market. Ah! that will be good," and she rubbed her hands at the prospect of not having to crouch under a leaky awning when the rain came pelting down, or over a tiny fire in a brass bowl in the winter, to thaw her frozen and benumbed hands.

Even the laborers in the fields, who were mainly dull-witted people with no learning whatsoever, heard the news; and they actually pondered over it and wondered whether it meant that they would never more be hungry and wretchedly clad.

One who thought deeply was a shepherd lad. He loved to bask lazily in the sun, to listen to the birds chirruping, and to all the sounds of the air and the fields and the forests. He seemed to understand them; the murmuring of the brooks on a warm day was like a gentle cradle song lulling him to sleep; on a day when the wind howled, its sulky growl as it dashed over the stones warned him that floods might come, and that he must move his flocks to safer ground.

"I wonder," he mused, "if I shall learn to read the written word and even to pen it myself. I could then write the song of the brook and the birds, so that others should know it."

And musing thus, he fell asleep. He slept longer than usual, and when he awoke, he was alarmed to see that the sun had set. Darkness was falling fast, and he had his flock to see safely home. The cows and sheep had begun to collect themselves as a matter of habit, and it was their noise that woke him. They were already trudging the well-known route, and all he had to do in following was to see that none strayed, or tumbled into the brook.

All went well until he came in sight of home. Then a huge bird, a ziz, bigger than several houses, appeared in the sky and swooped down on the cows and sheep.

The shepherd beat the monster off as long as he could with a big stick, while the affrighted animals scampered hastily homeward. The ziz however, was evidently determined not to be balked of its prey. It dug its talons deep into the flanks of an ox that had stampeded in the wrong direction and was lagging behind the others.

The poor animal bellowed in pain, and the shepherd, rushing to the rescue, seized it by the forelegs as it was being raised from the ground. Curling his leg round the slender trunk of a tree, the young man began a struggle with the ziz. The mighty bird, its eyes glowing like two signal lamps, tried to strike at him with his tremendous beak, one stroke of which would have been fatal.

In the fast gathering darkness it missed, fortunately for the shepherd, but the thrust of the beak caught the upper part of the tree trunk. It snapped under the blow, and the shepherd was compelled to release his hold. He still gripped tightly the forelegs of the ox, but with naught now to hold it back, the great bird had no difficulty in rising into the air. Before he fully grasped what had happened, the shepherd found himself high above the trees.

To release his hold would have meant destruction. He held on grimly, clutching the legs of the ox with all his might, and even swinging tip his feet to grip the hind-legs of the animal.

Higher and higher the ziz rose into the air, spreading its vast wings majestically, and flying silently and swiftly over the land. It made the shepherd giddy to glance down at the ground scurrying rapidly past far below him. So he closed his eyes, but opening them again for a moment, he was horrified to notice that the bird was now flying over the sea on which the moon was shining with silvery radiance. With a heavy sigh he gave himself up for lost, and began to consider whether it would be better to release his hold and fall down and be drowned, rather than be devoured by the gigantic bird.

Before he could make up his mind, the bird stopped, and the shepherd was bumped down on something with such violence that for a moment he was stunned. Looking around, when he re-gained his senses, he saw that he was on the top of a tower in the sea. Beside him was the carcass of the ox. Above them stood the ziz, its eyes glowing like twin fires, its beak thrust down to strike.

With a quick movement, the shepherd drew a knife which he carried in his girdle, and struck at the opening of the descending beak. The bird uttered a shrill cry of pain as the knife pierced its tongue, and in a few moments it had disappeared in the air. So swift was its flight that almost instantly it was a mere speck in the moonlit sky.

Thoroughly exhausted, the shepherd slept until awakened by the sound of a voice. Opening his eyes, he saw that the sun had risen. Above him stood a woman of ravishing beauty. He sprang to his feet and bowed low.

"Who are you?" asked Princess Solima, for she it was. "And tell me how came you here with this carcass of an ox, so distant from the land, so high up as this tower in the sea?"

"Of a truth I scarcely know," answered the shepherd. "It may be that I am bewitched, or dreaming, for my adventure passes all belief," and he related it.

The princess made no comment, but motioned to him that he should follow her. He did so and she placed food before him. He was ravenously hungry and did full justice to the meal. Then she led him to the bath chamber.

"Wash and robe thyself," she said, giving him some clothes, "and then I have much to inquire of thee."

The shepherd felt ever so much better when he had bathed, and then attired in the strange garments she had given him, he appeared before the princess.

She gazed at him so long and searchingly that he blushed in confusion.

"Thou art fair to look upon and of manly stature," said the princess.

The shepherd could only stammer a reply, but after a while he said, "Fair lady, who and what thou art I know not. Such beauty as thine is the right of princesses only. I am but a poor shepherd."

"And may not a shepherd be handsome?" she asked. "Tell me: who hath laid down a law that only royal personages may be fair to behold? I have seen princes of vile countenance."

She stopped suddenly, for she did not wish to betray her secret. They sat in a little room in the tower, unknown to the many guards down below, and, although the shepherd protested, the princess waited on him herself, bringing him food, and cushions on which he could rest that night.

Next morning they ascended the tower together.

"I come here every morning," said the princess.

"Why?" the shepherd asked.

"To see if my husband cometh," was the answer.

"Who is he?" asked the shepherd.

The princess laughed.

"I know not," she said. "Some mornings when I have stood here and grieved at my loneliness, I have felt inclined to make a vow that I would marry the first man who came hither."

The shepherd was silent. Then he looked boldly into the princess' eyes and said: "Thou hast told me I am the first man who has come to thee. I am emboldened to declare my love for thee, a feeling that swept over me the moment my eyes beheld thee. Who thou art, what thou art, I know not, I care not. Shall we be husband and wife?"

The princess gave him her hand.

"It is ordained," she said, and thus their troth was plighted.

"We cannot remain here forever," said the princess, presently. "Canst thou, husband of my heart's choice, devise some means of escape?"

He looked down at the carcass of the ox thoughtfully for a few moments.

"I have it," he exclaimed, excitedly. "It is a safe assumption that the monster bird that brought me will return for his meal. He can then carry us away. If the heavens approve," he said, fervently, "thus it shall be."

That very night the ziz returned and feasted on the ox, and while it was fully occupied appeasing its hunger, the shepherd managed to attach strong ropes to its legs. To this he attached a large basket in which he and his bride made themselves comfortable with cushions. Nor did they forget to take a store of food.

Toward morning the ziz rose slowly into the air, and the lovers clutched each other tightly as the basket spun round and round. The giant bird did not seem to notice its burden at all, and after a moment it began a swift flight over the sea. After many hours a city became visible, and as it was approached the shepherd could note the excitement caused by the appearance of the ziz. The bird was getting tired, and having at last noticed the weight tied to its feet was evidently seeking to get rid of it.

Flying low it dashed the basket against a tower. The occupants feared they might be killed, but suddenly the cords snapped, the basket rested on the parapet of the tower, and the bird flew swiftly away.

No sooner had the shepherd extricated himself and his bride from the basket, than armed guards appeared. At sight of the princess they lowered their weapons and fell upon their faces.

"Inform my father I have returned," she said, and they immediately rose to do her bidding.

"Know you where you are?" asked the shepherd.

"Yes; this is the king's palace," was the reply.

Soon the king appeared, and with almost hysterical joy he embraced his daughter.

"I am happy to see thee again," he cried. "I crave thy pardon for immuring thee in the sea fortress. Thou shalt tell me all thy adventures."

Then he caught sight of the shepherd.

"Who is this?" he demanded.

"Thy son-in-law, my husband," said the princess, her joy showing in her bright eyes.

"What prince art thou?" asked the king.

"A prince among men," answered the princess quickly. "A man without riches, who comes from the people and will teach us their needs and how to rule them."

The king bowed to the inevitable. He blessed his son-in-law and daughter, appointed them to rule over a province, and they settled down to make everybody thoroughly happy, contented and prosperous.

Taken from *Jewish Fairy Tales And Legends* by "Aunt Naomi" (Gertrude Landa) New York: Bloch Publishing Co., Inc. "The

Jewish Book Concern" [1919]. NOTICE OF ATTRIBUTION Scanned at sacred-texts.com, March 2005. Proofed and formatted by John Bruno Hare. This text is in the public domain in the US because it was published prior to 1922. These files may be used for any non-commercial purpose, provided this notice of attribution is left intact in all copies.

# Appendix: The Baal Shem Tov – Rabbi, Religious Formulator, or Shaman?

By considering the upbringing, apprenticeship, practices and beliefs of Yisrael Ben Eliezer, later known as The Baal Shem Tov (The Master of the Good Name), it will be shown how in many respects it might be more accurate to refer to him as a shaman rather than a rabbi. Although he is mainly known in world Jewry for being the founder of the Hasidic movement, it will be argued that it was above all the shamanic attributes the Baal Shem Tov possessed that led to him having such a profound influence on his own and succeeding generations.

As Tatiana Bulgakova points out,

> Shamanism is an extremely flexible phenomenon and is able to adapt in a changing situation. It is able to find its way between the opposite ideological systems like atheism and shamanism. The stability of shamanic mythology and ritual tradition is quite relative because the concepts of the spiritual world and the methods of communicating with them are deeply individual for each shaman. These skills are created and learned through the personal experience of an individual shaman. This variability determines the high degree of flexibility of shamanism and its capacity to change relatively easily under the impact of cultural shifts. The

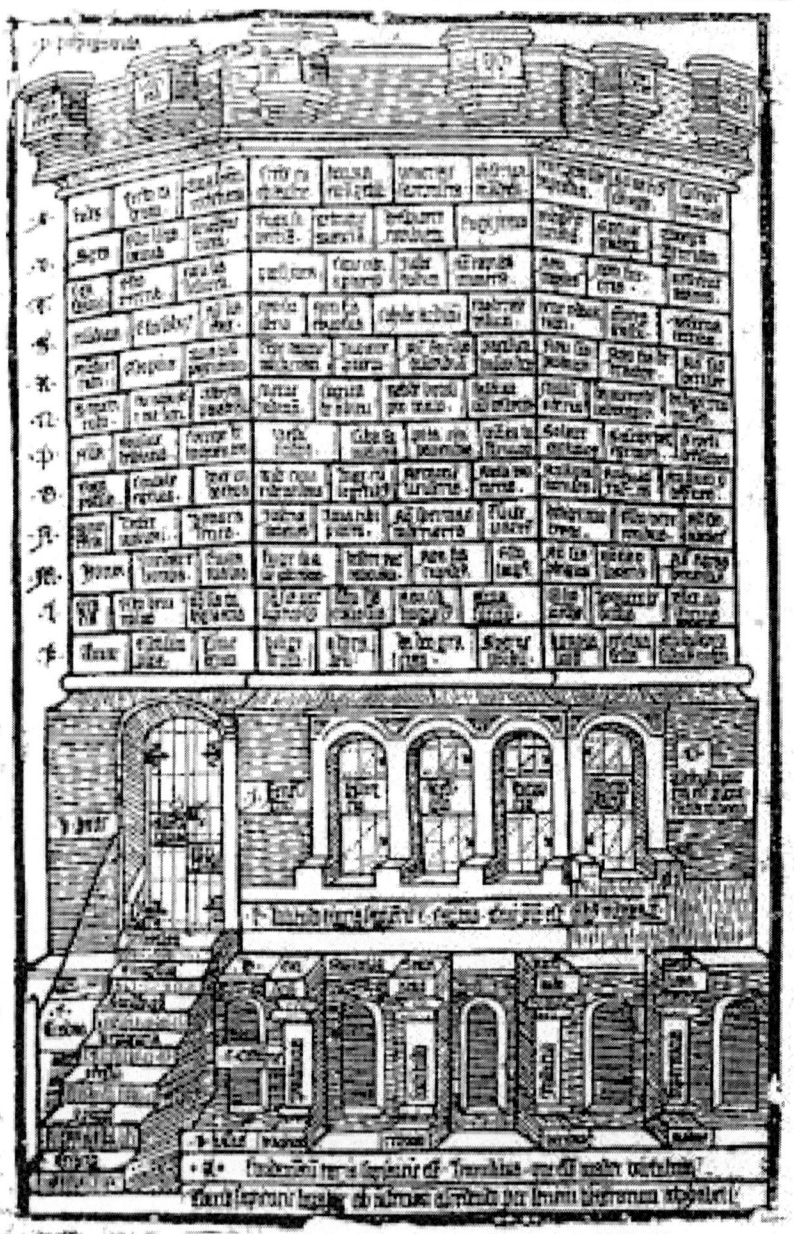

The Tower of Wisdom, Nurmberg 1470

substitution of shaman drums with pans and pot lids, the possibility of concealing one's true convictions by putting on a mask of a member of the party, and the fundamental perception about the possibility of accomplishing the same 'shamanic' tasks using very different means (as there is no fundamental difference whether the shaman uses a drum or a *withe*[1] – all these are manifestations of the same characteristics of shamanism). These are the various manifestations of shamanism's ability to take a large number of forms, without altering its core essence (Bulgakova, 2009, p.95).

Similarly, as we shall see, the Baal Shem Tov showed Judaism could be a flexible phenomenon too, in that he was able to adapt it to suit the times he was living in so as to ensure its practice both survived and flourished.

First of all, however, what are claimed to be the biographical details of the life of Rabbi Israel Baal Shem Tov (The Besht) 18 Elul 5458 - 6 Sivan 5520 (1698-1760). These can be found on the website of the Baal Shem Tov Foundation, and are presented below by way of an introduction.

> Yisrael Ben Eliezer, later known as The Baal Shem Tov (The Master of the Good Name), was born on the 18th of Elul 5458 (August 27, 1698) to Rabbi Eliezer and his wife Sarah. They lived in the small village of Okup on the Russian Polish border. Both Rabbi Eliezer and Sarah were already very old when their first child Srulik (Israel) was born.
>
> The days passed quickly and when Srulik was only five

years old, his father Rabbi Eliezer died. The last words his father said to him were "Israel my son, you have a very holy soul, don't fear anything but God". Soon thereafter, his mother Sarah also died.

Young Israel, now an orphan, was adopted by the local community and educated as was common in Jewish communities at that time. That is, he probably learned to read Hebrew by four, to translate the Bible from the original at five, and began Talmud at about eight. By the time he entered his teens, he was probably fluent in both Bible and Talmud.

The tradition is that young Israel was different from other children. He would often go into fields and woods and mountains, spending many hours alone, speaking to God. Not having parents, it's not surprising he would go into nature to seek out his Father in Heaven. At an early age he was aware of the presence of God in all aspects of life.

Like Solomon, he is said to have learned the languages of the animals and birds (Buxbaum, 2005, p.44), and knowledge of this secret language was also one of the attributes that the indigenous shaman was traditionally said to possess.

The ability to understand the language of the animals and to be able to communicate with them has in fact long been valued by Jewish mystics. This should come as no surprise, though, to anyone familiar with the Old Testament. For we are told in the Book of Job (35:11) that God "teaches us through the beasts of the earth, and makes us wise through the birds of the skies", and in the Book of Ecclesiastes (3:19) we learn that "Both you and they [the animals] share the same life breath of the Creator, and neither of you is any more important to Creator than the other." The Baal Shem Tov was supposedly no stranger to this knowledge either, for he 'taught that the divine Presence dwells in the life of all four beings, the Still Beings (stones, planets), the Sprouting Beings (grasses, trees), the Wild Beings (animals, fish, insects, birds), and the Talking beings (humans)' (Winkler, 2003, pp.163-164).

When Israel entered his teens, the community's responsibility for him ended and he had to begin supporting himself. First, he was hired as a school assistant because of his way with children. He was known to sing psalms and other songs with the children as they walked to school. He would also tell the children stories and teach them how to pray.

Israel's next position was that of a caretaker at the local synagogue. His main duties were to clean the synagogue and arrange the books. This gave him the time to study and develop. Late at night, when everyone was gone from the study hall of the synagogue, he would study the large tomes of the Talmud, Midrash and Jewish Law. Probably, he also studied Kabbalah, as was common in those days. He developed a great expertise in these areas. This expertise was later spoken about by his students and appeared in his teachings. Young Israel was said to sleep during the day when he had nothing to do. The local people thought he was not very smart.

Rabbi Adam Baal Shem[2], the leader of the hidden tzaddikim at this time, "was in possession of a hand-written manuscript of a book that contained the deepest secrets of the Kabbalah, including the practical Kabbalah – how to use divine Names to perform miracles" (Buxbaum, 2005, p.36) and he was told, in answer to a dream question, to give it to the son of Rabbi Eliezer in the town of Okup in Poland. The sacred tome was given to Israel by Rabbi Adam's son, who became his student. Rabbi Adam's son, however, died soon after, and Israel then moved to a little town near Brody.

> There he was employed as a teacher of young children. He became acquainted with Rabbi Ephraim of Brody who became aware of Israel's spiritual greatness. Right before Rabbi Ephraim's death, the Rabbi arranged for the engagement of Israel to his daughter Chana.
>
> When Israel came to Rabbi Gershon of Kitov, Rabbi Ephraim's son, requesting the hand of his fiancée, Rabbi Gershon thinking that Israel was a peasant, tried to throw him out. But, when Israel produced a letter of engagement signed by Rabbi Ephriam, he called Chana and asked her opinion. After Israel spoke with Chana, no doubt telling her who he really was, she agreed to the match. Even though Rabbi Gershon disapproved of the match, he allowed them to marry and sent them away with a horse and wagon.
>
> The bride and groom moved to a mountain village called Kutty between Kitov and Kasov in the Carpathian Mountains. This little village was also not far from Brody. Israel spent the next ten years praying and studying with an angelic mentor, Ahiyah ha-Shiloni ... [who] initiated Israel into the mysteries of the Torah.

Ahiyah ha-Shiloni ... was a disciple of Moses and among those who made the Exodus from Egypt and was present at the splitting of the Red Sea. He was at the giving of the Torah at Sinai and sat in the religious court of David the King of Israel. He was the master and teacher of Elijah, the heavenly teacher of the mystics, and of Rabbi Shimon bar Yohai, the great mystic and author of the Zohar (Buxbaum, 2005, p.90).

Incidentally, it was Ahiya ha-Shiloni who was later to tell the Baal Shem Tov, on his thirty-sixth birthday, that the time had come for his light to be revealed in the sight of all Israel. The Baal Shem Tov, however, resisted his master's request. His struggle "against becoming the unique leader of Israel, was similar to the struggle of Moses – who did not want to accept the holy mission of being Israel's redeemer from the Egyptian exile (Buxbaum, 2005, p.106). It was also typical of the initial resistance to follow the "call" shown by those chosen to be future shamans.

> For a time, [after he got married] Israel was a shochet (ritual slaughterer) and teacher in Koslovitz. Israel and Chana had two children, Edel and Tzvi Hirsch. [The latter, on his death, became his successor].

> Rabbi Israel first revealed himself to the world on Lag BaOmer, 5585 (May 22, 1734). Then Rabbi Israel moved to Talust and became famous as a holy man. Next he moved to Medzibusch in Western Ukraine for the remainder of his life.

> In Medzibusch[3], his fame spread and students attached themselves to him. Not only were ordinary people attracted

to him, but some of the greatest Rabbinical luminaries also joined with him.

Although very few documents written by Rabbi Israel still exist, many stories and teachings have been passed down to the present time. He became known as the Baal Shem Tov – the Master of the Good Name.

As Rabbi Israel's fame spread, so did an opposition (Misnagdim) begin to grow.

Being a living legend, the Baal Shem Tov spent most of his time in worship, serving God, teaching his disciples, and giving blessings to the thousands that came to see him.

The Baal Shem Tov passed away on Shavuos, 5520 (May 23, 1760) having founded the Hasidic movement that lives on today (taken from http://www.baalshemtov.com/whowashe.htm [accessed 3/3/09]).

It has been said that "When the Baal Shem Tov reached the height of his influence, his movement numbered tens of thousands of followers and scores of disciples, many of them great rabbis and scholars. His authority had grown and become established to such an extent that he appointed and removed rabbis, *maggadim* (preachers), *shochtim*, and cantors in many towns and villages" (Buxbaum, 2005, p.288).

However, was Hasidism actually "his movement"? In fact, Hasidism ... was an outgrowth of an already existing religious orientation and not, as many have suggested, a radically new phenomenon that came as history's response to a crisis of Judaism or of Jewish society. Hasidism was probably connected to the growing popularisation of mysticism inspired in large part by the example of the traditional mystical-ascetic Hasidim and ba'lai shem and made it practicable through the spread of inexpensive, unsophisticated Kabbalah-based literature ... It made every Jew into a candidate for Hasid, by abolishing the daunting ascetic requirements and obliging the leader of the group, the zaddik, to focus his efforts on the individual (Rosman, 1996, p.39).

It soon becomes apparent that the accuracy of much of the information we have about the Baal Shem Tov is questionable, for the little biographical information concerning him that does exist is so interwoven with legends that in many cases it is hard to arrive at the historical facts. Much of what is believed about the Ba'al Shem Tov is based on stories that were compiled in *Shivhei Ha-Besht* (In Praise of the Besht) more than a generation after his death, and the descriptions that we do have of him and his feats, written by others, are more often than not overshadowed by the describers' own ideological proclivities. The *Shivhei Ha-Besht*, for example, has been described as a collection of stories "designed to legitimize the Besht by placing him in a chain of mystical tradition" (Rosman, 1996, p.145). In other words, it is nothing more than a work of hagiography, a proof text, not written to record the biography of the Besht, but to persuade its readers to accept a particular doctrine. Another problem is that as far as we know, the Baal Shem Tov produced no written works. As Rosman (1996) points out, there are in fact only four sources that can be reasonably considered to be reliable copies of documents originating from the Besht himself – the Holy epistle, a letter to Jacob Joseph, a passage in the responsum of Meir of Konstantynów, and a letter to Rabbi Moses of Kutów.

However, what we do know is that Besht settled as a teacher at Flust near Brody where, on account of his recognized honesty and his knowledge of human nature,

> he was chosen to act as arbitrator and mediator for people conducting suits against each other [just as the indigenous shaman of a community would frequently do]; and his services were brought into frequent requisition owing to the fact that the Jews had their own civil courts in Poland. In this avocation Besht succeeded in making so deep an impression upon the rich and learned Ephraim of Kuty that the latter promised Besht his daughter Anna in marriage
>
> (http://www.jewishencyclopedia.com/view.jsp?letter=B&artid=18 [accessed 3/3/09]).

We also know that during the many years that Besht lived in the village called Kutty in the Carpathian Mountains, he learned how to use plants for healing purposes, and his first appearance in public was as an ordinary Baal Shem. A Baal Shem, a "Master of the Divine Names",

> was a combination of a practical kabbalist who cured by means of prayers, amulets, and incantations using holy Names; and a popular healer familiar with such common techniques as bleeding by lancet or leeches, *segulot* (mystically potent items or techniques), and remedies concocted from animal, vegetable, and mineral matter. *Baal shems* were considered especially effective in expelling dybbuks, evil spirits, and other demons (Buxbaum, 2005, p.359).

As for the ways in which the holy Names can be used,

> The various permutations of the various Sacred Names can … effect or rearrange the "natural order" of things, since the natural order of things and their makeup are animated by Creator whose creative essence is concealed within its many Names. The kabbalistic rite of the permutation of the sacred Names would then be like rearranging molecules with the intention of altering their structures to effect any variety of manifestations (Winkler, 2003, pp.69-70).

Acting as a healer, as the Baal Shem Tov did, was also how the indigenous shaman traditionally contributed to the community in which he lived.

The parallels between the way of the shaman as described by Eliade and that of the typical Baal Shem have been noted by Moshe Rosman in some detail:

> Ba'alei Shem share many of the characteristics of what Mircea Eliade dubbed "shaman," an ancient type of holy man appearing in various forms in many of the world's religions up until modern times The shaman is a master of the techniques of ecstasy, whose soul, during his trances, passes from one cosmic region to another: ascending to the realm of the holy, descending to the netherworld, and communicating with the spirits. His ability to move beyond the world of physical experience makes him a specialist in matters of the human soul. He can see the soul, discerning when it is possessed by spirits or wanders away from its rightful place in the body. The shaman can liberate a

possessed soul or chase an errant one and return it to its normal state. Such liberation is manifested in exorcism, while restoration of the soul is seen as curing of illness. Often the shaman serves as a psychopomp who conducts souls to the afterworld (Rosman, p.13).

Ba'alei Shem, from ancient times through the seventeenth and eighteenth centuries, fit Eliade's typology in many respects. They were ecstatic mystics whose main technique in communicating with the supernatural was the magical employment of the names of God, particularly as written in inscriptions placed in amulets (Rosman, 1996, p.14).

Not only has the shaman traditionally played the role of a healer, such practices have also had a considerable influence on contemporary forms of healing. "Specific techniques long used in shamanism, such as change in state of consciousness, stress-reduction, visualisation, positive thinking, and assistance from non-ordinary sources, are some of the approaches now widely employed in contemporary holistic practice" (Harner, 1990, p. xiii). Jungian and Gestalt therapists also use guided visualisation with their patients to enable them to access inner wisdom. This often involves the patient having a dialogue with an inner sage or teacher in which he / she is encouraged to ask whatever questions seem to be most helpful, and the process can be compared to the shaman's journey to find a spirit teacher (see Walsh, 1990, p.132).

Contrary to what might be expected, shamanism and sorcery are not necessarily "anti-ethical to the Hebrew scriptures ... The proscriptions in the Bible against divination and sorcery refer specifically to the kinds of sorcery practised by specific cultures whose ways the Jewish people were forbidden to emulate" (Winkler, 2003, p.3). Winkler then goes on to suggest that the Jewish scriptural verse in the Book of Exodus 22:17 can be literally translated as

> "You should not sustain a witch," meaning don't get into the habit of supporting the livelihood of the village magician; don't let some guy with a lot of supernatural power drain you of your savings through fear and intimidation. Let him do a job like everybody else, and perform his magic out of the goodness of his heart and in recognition of the sacred gift he possesses (Winkler, 2003, p.3)

This is, however, surely what Winkler would like the verse to be translated as, rather than what it was necessarily intended to imply, and is surely taking the original argument one step too far.

The person traditionally chosen to be the shaman of a community was often a wounded healer—someone who had been through a near-death experience and who was consequently well suited to helping others through difficult times in their lives. The experience would establish the healer's warrant to minister to his people's needs as one who knew how to control disorder. The profession to which the concept of the wounded healer most aptly applies today is probably that of the psychoanalyst and the kind of shamanism that has been practised by tribal peoples through the ages can thus be viewed as a form of pre-scientific psychotherapy (see Lewis, 2003, p.172).

Although emphasis, especially in neo-shamanism, is often placed on the healing of individual illness, either psychological or physical, it should be remembered that another role the shaman was traditionally called on to lay was in the healing of the community.

In his work as a healer, what the Baal Shem Tov, like the shaman, did not do was to make use of his own power. "Everyone who came to tell him of the success of his treatment or to thank him for a miracle he had wrought was asked to thank God, blessed be He, because, said the Besht, "Everything that happens is in God's hands and it's God, blessed be He, who puts miraculous powers in medicinal herbs and amulets; it's God, blessed be He, who answers prayers and fulfils a tzaddik's blessings" (Buxbaum, 2005, p.123).

Now let us consider what it was exactly that made Besht stand out from his contemporaries and marked him out as being different. It is generally agreed that

> ... The foundation-stone of ?asidism as laid by Besht is a strongly marked pantheistic conception of God. He declared the whole universe, mind and matter, to be a manifestation of the Divine Being; that this manifestation is not an emanation from God, as is the conception of the Cabala, for nothing can be separated from God: all things are rather forms in which He reveals Himself. When man speaks, said Besht, he should remember that his speech is an element of life, and that life itself is a manifestation of God. Even evil exists in God. This seeming contradiction is explained on the ground that evil is not bad in itself, but only in its relation to man. It is wrong to look with desire upon a woman; but it is divine to admire her beauty: it is wrong only in so far as man does not regard beauty as a manifestation of God, but misconceives it, and thinks of it in reference to himself. Nevertheless, sin is nothing positive, but is identical with the imperfections of human deeds and thought. Whoever does not believe that God resides in all things, but separates Him and them in his

thoughts, has not the right conception of God. It is equally fallacious to think of a creation in time: creation, that is, God's activity, has no end. God is ever active in the changes of nature: in fact, it is in these changes that God's continuous creativeness consists.

... Besht was a man of the people, who knew how to give his meta-physical conception of God an eminently practical significance [as, indeed, the shamanic practitioners of old did, who made it their business to deal with the everyday practical concerns of the members of the communities they lived in].

The first result of his principles was a remarkable optimism. Since God is immanent in all things, all things must possess something good in which God manifests Himself as the source of good. For this reason, Besht taught, every man must be considered good, and his sins must be explained, not condemned. ...Another important result of his doctrines, which was of great practical importance, was his denial that asceticism is pleasing to God. "Whoever maintains that this life is worthless is in error: it is worth a great deal; only one must know how to use it properly" ... He considered care of the body as necessary as care of the soul; since matter is also a manifestation of God, and must not be considered as hostile or opposed to Him (http://www.jewishencyclopedia.com/view.jsp?letter=B&artid=18 [accessed 3/3/09]).

Not only can most shamans be said to practise asceticism, at least during their initiations, if not throughout their lives, but the stories told about Besht's own retreat into the woods of the Carpathian mountains and his rejection of worldly goods can actually be interpreted as an example of asceticism too. Therefore, this is a concept that needs to be considered in more detail.

It has been observed that no one can engage in a religious ceremony of any importance without submitting to a kind of preparatory initiation that introduces him gradually into the sacred world. This can take the form of anointing, purifications, and blessings–all essentially positive operations. But the same result can be achieved through fasts, vigils, retreat, and silence, that is by ritual abstinences that are nothing more than the practical application of specific prohibitions (Durkheim, 2001, p.230). To abstain from something that is useful or that answers to some human need clearly entails discomfort, and this becomes asceticism proper when practised as a way of life. Normally the negative cult serves only as a form of preparation for the positive cult, and an example of this would be the rites of puberty or the initiatory rites that the apprentice shaman has to undergo. And it is of course not only the goals pursued by apprentice shamans that call for ascetic practices to bring about transmutation–the same is required of other mystics too, such as yogis.

According to James, asceticism symbolizes "the belief that there is an element of real wrongness in this world, which is neither to be ignored nor evaded, but which must be squarely met and overcome by an appeal to the soul's heroic resources, and neutralized and cleansed away by suffering" (James, 1982, p.362). However, for initiates it has no such symbolism. It is merely their apprenticeship, part of a necessary process before they can become accepted by both their teachers and the people they will ultimately represent. The tales told about the Baal Shem Tov's withdrawal from life in the town to spending most of his time in the woods can be regarded as an example of such practice. Therefore it is not in fact at odds with his rejection of asceticism as a way of life.

What Besht objected to was the emphasis the rabbis of his day placed on the study of the Talmud, while almost entirely neglecting the growth of man's inner life.

> Besht laid all the stress on prayer. "All that I have achieved," he once remarked, "I have achieved not through study, but through prayer." Prayer, however, is not petitioning God to grant a request, though that is one end of prayer, but ("cleaving")—the feeling of oneness with God, the state of the soul when man gives up the consciousness of his separate existence, and joins himself to the eternal being of God. Such a state produces a species of indescribable joy (which is a necessary ingredient of the true worship of God.
>
> ... His teachings concerning "joy") were especially opposed to asceticism. The followers of Luria considered weeping an indispensable accompaniment to prayer; while Besht considered weeping and feelings of sorrow to be wholly objectionable. The sinner who repents of his sin should not sorrow over the past, but should rejoice over the Heavenly Voice, over the Divine Power, working within him and enabling him to recognize the true in admitting his sin. The function of joy in prayer is paralleled by glowing enthusiasm and ecstasy = "to become inflamed") in every act of worship. Fear of God is only an initiatory step to

real worship, which must spring from a love of God and a surrender of self to Him. In his enthusiasm man will not think either of this life or of the next: the feeling of union with God is in itself a means and an end. Enthusiasm, however, demands progress, not the mere fulfilment of the Law's precepts in a daily routine, which becomes deadening: true religion consists in an ever-growing recognition of God (http://www.jewishencyclopedia.com/view.jsp?letter=B&artid=18 [accessed 3/3/09]).

In a letter the Besht sent to Rabbi Jacob Joseph of Polonne there is "a clear and reliable statement of the Besht's anti-ascetism. Having been informed of Jacob Joseph's intention to fast, the Besht attempted to convince him not to do so and even ordered him to refrain from this unhealthy practice. Simultaneously, the Besht provided an alternative means – attachment to the letters of study texts – of attaining the same spiritual result that was to be achieved by fasting (Rosman, 1996, p.115).

Shamans, whether chosen by Superhuman Beings or whether they themselves seek to attract their attention and obtain their favours, can be defined as specialists in the sacred who succeed in having mystical experiences which are expressed in the shaman's trance. Consequently, they can be regarded as primarily ecstatics who learn, through their initiation, how to orient themselves in the other regions which they enter during trance and how to explore the new planes of existence which are thus revealed to them (see Eliade, 2003, p.95). It should be noted, however, that not all shamans have this ability and genuine ecstatic shamanism needs to be differentiated from both the imitative and demonstrative forms referred to by Hultrantz. As Eliade recognised, the attraction of the ecstatic state is that it is a means of transcending the profane, individual condition and attaining a transpersonal perspective:

Whether there is a re-immersion in primordial life in order to obtain a spiritual renewal of the entire being or (as in Buddhist mysticism and Eskimo shamanism) a deliverance from the illusions of the flesh, the result is the same—a certain recovery of the very source of spiritual existence, which is at once "truth" and "life" (Eliade, 1989, p.64). And in our urban jungles where stress is endemic in that it has become a way of life, it is just this sort of spiritual renewal that people hunger for.

Besht was of the opinion that true worship, as above explained, the cleaving to, and the unification with, God.

> To use his own words, "the ideal of man is to be a revelation himself, clearly to recognize himself as a manifestation of God." Mysticism, he said, is not the Cabala, which every one may learn; but that sense of true oneness, which is usually as strange, unintelligible, and incomprehensible to mankind as dancing is to a dove. The man, however, who is capable of this feeling is endowed with a genuine intuition; and it is the perception of such a man which is called prophecy, or "bat ?ol," according to the degree of his insight. From this it results, in the first place, that the "?addi?," the ideal man, may lay claim to authority equal, in a certain sense, to the authority of the Prophets. A second and more important result of the doctrine is that the ?addi?, through his oneness with God, forms a connecting-link between the Creator and creation (http://www.jewishencyclopedia.com/view.jsp?letter=B&artid=18 [accessed 3/3/09]).

The *tzaddik* has been compared to a ferryman "who can enable one to traverse the turbulent waters of this world, the *ish haElokim*, the Godly man, who … is uniquely empowered to bring man closer to God, and God closer to man" (Sears, 1997, p.xxiv). For the Baal Shem Tov, the way to achieve this was through *deveykus*, mystical communion with God. As for the society of hidden tzaddikim, this was

> a movement of mystics who rejected the aloof attitude of a religious establishment that focused on the external aspect of Torah scholarship and religion and looked down on the uneducated and imperfectly observant simple people. … Instead they "taught simple working Jews the basics of Judaism with an emphasis on *musar* (character development and ethics) (Buxbaum, 2005, p.13).

The hidden tzaddikim also sought to "enter heaven while alive" [in the same way Elijah the Prophet is said to have done] – "to experience godly reality during their lifetime – by means of a fiery devotion to the mystic path" (Buxbaum, 2005, p.29). As for Elijah the Prophet, he is said to have first revealed himself to Israel on his sixteenth birthday. We are informed that from then on "the angelic prophet appeared to the Baal Shem Tov regularly and became his foremost teacher" (Buxbaum, 2005, p.30).

We are told that when the Baal Shem Tov prayed

> he was completely immersed in the spiritual world. He lost awareness of his body and the material world, so that he could not even speak. … He often stood praying for hours at a time. His d'vekut then was exalted and total. Sometimes his face burned like a torch; at other times, his

eyes streamed nonstop with tears of joy. He often leaped and danced while davvening. In the morning, when he put on tefillin and recited the Shema, his mind and thoughts elevated, and he sometimes ran around the synagogue as if he was in another world (Buxbaum, 2005, p.126).

We are also reliably informed that while praying, "he often trembled and shook uncontrollably" (Buxbaum, 2005, p.127), in much the same manner as a shaman would do when entering a trancelike state. Indeed, to an outsider, it would probably have been difficult to differentiate between the two in this respect.

The Hebrew word for "prophet" was *nahb* – "one who is called". The prophet was a person called by God to be the bearer of his message to men. And as his life was wholly dedicated to serving God, he was often referred to as "the man of God". According to the biblical accounts of prophets such as Moses, Jonah, Jeremiah and Isaiah, the vocation would come to the prophet spontaneously, and often contrary to both expectation and desire (see Moscati, 1957, p.139). In a similar way, the call to be a shaman was often contrary to expectation and desire and, like the prophet, he would fight against it.

The following account of the attributes of the Hebrew prophet make the resemblance between him / her and the traditional shaman even more apparent:

> The *nahvee* was capable of bringing to the people what they themselves were often not able to access. Some of that was seeing into the future, but that was not all of it or was it the most essential aspect of what the *nahvee* brought. More importantly, the *nahvee* brought clarity when things were muddled, vision when things got foggy, hope when it

looked like there would be no tomorrow. Not unlike the Native American medicine carrier, the *nahvee* in ancient Judea would receive her or his vision during an extended period of solitude in the wilderness, often without food or water, and would then return to the community to share the vision (Winkler, 2003, pp.42-43).

In his paper *Shamanistic Features in the Old Testament*, Arvid Kapelrud describes how

> The *nabbi* ... were active at Canaanite cult places, where they used to gather in flocks. They used different means to bring themselves into ecstasy: harp, tambourine, flute and lyre are mentioned in I Sam. X: 5. When the spirit came upon them, they prophesied and it is even so expressed that they were "turned into another man" (I Sam. X: 6) ...When the king needed divine assistance to start a new task, e.g. a war, he used to call his *nabbi*, as it is told in the O.T. about King Ahab in the 9th century B.C., I Kings XXII (in Edsman, 1967, p.91).

Despite the fact that the *nabbi* phenomenon in Israel was of Canaanite origin and was never fully accepted by the most orthodox, at the same time everyone must surely have been familiar with such practices. Moreover, a strong case can be made for the fact that such shamanistic practices had an influence on biblical literature–the Book of Jonah being a prime example.

Although prophets and other mystics with a direct experience of God or the spirits are often crucial in the early stages of the development of a world religion, they later become regarded as a threat–a challenge to the established authority. This can be seen, for example, in the Christian Church, which has tended to suppress or marginalize this kind of practice, as has Orthodox Judaism (see Vitebsky, 2001, p.134). A good example of this can be seen in the way that the approach of the Baal Shem Tov was rejected by the Talmudists.

> ... Besht ... laid stress upon a religious spirit, and not upon the forms of religion. Though he considered the Law to be holy and inviolable, he held that one's entire life should be a service of God, and that this would constitute true worship of Him. Since every act in life is a manifestation of God, and must perforce be divine, it is man's duty so to live that the things called "earthly" may also become noble and pure, that is, divine. Besht tried to realize his ideal in his own career. ... [H]is distinguishing traits were a merciful judgment of others, fearlessness combined with dislike of strife, and a boundless joy in life.

> ...He was certainly not a scholar; ... [and he] was still less gifted as a speaker. But the lack of scholarship and oratory was supplied by fine satire and inventiveness in telling parables. There are many satirical remarks directed against his opponents, an especially characteristic one being his designation of the typical Talmudist of his day as "a man who through sheer study of the Law has no time to think about God." (http://www.jewishencyclopedia.com/view.jsp?letter=B&artid=18 [accessed 3/3/09]).

One of the things that the Baal Shem Tov was apparently able to do was to "make Unifications through a story. When he saw the supernal channels were corrupted and it was impossible to rectify them with prayer, he would rectify and unify them with a story" (Shulman, 1993, p.73).

Incidentally, Rebbe Nachman of Bratzlav (1772-1810), the great-grandson of the Baal Shem Tov, was also a storyteller of considerable skill. When Rabbi Nachman began telling stories, he said clearly, "I will start telling stories." His meaning was that since he hadn't succeeded in bringing people close to God with his lessons, he would do so with his stories (Schulman. 1993, p.73). He is also quoted as having remarked: "People say that stories are good for putting one to sleep. But I say that through stories, people can be woken up from their sleep" (Shulman, 1993, p.74).

One of the traditional roles of the shaman was that of a storyteller too. The shaman's journey is followed by his / her account of the experience–the story of the ascent to the Upper World or the decent to the world below, how the spirits encountered along the way were dealt with, and how the return was achieved. And, as Eliade noted, "Probably a large number of epic "subjects" or motifs, as well as many characters, images, and clichés of epic literature ... were borrowed from the narratives of shamans describing their journeys and adventures in the superhuman worlds" (Eliade, 1989, p.510). Evidence to support this claim can be found in the biblical story of Jonah, for example (see Berman, 2007), which can be interpreted as a spiritual journey to the Lower World, or the ascent to the Upper World in the fairy tale *Jack and the Beanstalk*.

A cosmology serves to orient a community to its world by defining the place of its people in the universal scheme of things. It tells the members of the community who they are and where they stand in relation to the rest of creation (see Mathews, 1994, p.12). Such cosmologies are presented in the stories that are told by shamans in that they account for the origin and nature of the world and so help us to make sense of it. Moreover, the telling of such tales by the shaman confirms his / her mastery of the skills required to deal with the spirits and inspires the community's confidence. Through shamanistic imagery and rites, mythology can be seen to provide us with a sense of *numen* in relation to human existence and also to the universe:

> The organized structure of the cosmos offers comprehensible images, which help define a person's place within it, thus validating the social order and the very essence of society itself. Perhaps, more importantly, myths serve as guidelines for the individual, through the various crises and traumas arising from the need to conform to social mores, to lead a beneficial existence more or less in balance with the perennial cycles of the universe (Ripinsky-Naxon, 1993, p.194).

To this list, however, can be added the power of mythology to transform our lives and even, it can be argued, the social order itself. Myths can be regarded as fictional stories that originated in early human communities "to explain commonplace but mysterious events in the natural world ... based on the premise that one can somehow perceive and distinguish between *reality as it really is* ... and reality *as it happens to be (mis)represented*" (Braun & McCutcheon, 2000, p.190). At the same time, a myth can be seen to convey, in some veiled, encoded or symbolic form, a social group's deepest personal and social values, a viewpoint endorsed by Eliade. It is also, in the words of Doniger, "a story shared by a group of people who find [or "fabricate" as McCutcheon suggests] their most important meanings in it" (Braun & McCutcheon, 2000, p.2). It is thus apparent that as the mythologue of the community, the shaman's role is of great significance.

"Liminality, marginality and structural inferiority are conditions in which are frequently generated myths, symbols, rituals, philosophical systems, and works of art" (Turner, 1995, pp.128-9). It is during the liminal stage referred to by Turner that the shaman undertakes the "journey" and the account of the experience then follows. Turner sees this stage as a movement from structure to anti-structure. However, it can in fact be argued that the liminal stage has a structure of its own, just as the "journey" which takes place during the liminal stage does. Maddox, writing in the 1920s, clearly doubted the effectiveness of the shaman as an intermediary between the people and the higher powers, as can be seen from the quote that follows. But he did recognize the importance of the shaman as an educator:

> Whatever good he accomplished as physician and counsellor, his efforts in interceding with the higher powers were of course futile. But the medicine man gradually became the teacher of the young men of the nation, and the almoner of the race. Almost down to the present time, education and charity are largely in the hands of the religious class (Maddox, 2003, p.286).

As the Baal Shem Tov himself showed, it can be argued it is in this way, perhaps more effectively than in any other, that the shaman can have a significant role to play in society. After all, it is stories and the stories about him that he is now mainly remembered for. And we know that the Baal Shem Tov was well aware of the power of stories to bring about significant change: For example, he is reported to have said that "Whoever tells or listens to stories about tzaddikim, or even about ordinary people who at times rise to holiness, is as if engaged in the mystic study and meditation on the Divine Chariot – because the tzaddikim are the chariot, the vehicle for Godliness in the world" (Buxbaum, 2005, p.66).

> ... Much of Besht's success was also due to his firm conviction that God had entrusted him with a special mission to spread his doctrines. In his enthusiasm and ecstasy he believed that he often had heavenly visions revealing his mission to him. In fact, for him every intuition was a divine revelation; and divine messages were daily occurrences (http://www.jewishencyclopedia.com/view.jsp?letter=B&artid=18 [accessed 3/3/09]).

What are described above as "divine messages" bear a striking resemblance to the messages provided by the spirit helpers the shaman would encounter on his or her journeys in a trancelike state into other realities. Besht himself is claimed to have said that his teacher was Ahijah of Shiloh, the prophet who at God's bidding undertook to bring about the breach between Judah and Israel, and a teacher who seems to have played a similar role to that of the sacred teacher the shaman traditionally turns to for guidance.

The term "religious formulator" is used in the title of this work as the Baal Shem Tov can by no means be considered to have taken on the conventional role traditionally played by a rabbi. It has been shown that the Baal Shem Tov, like the shaman, was familiar with working in an ecstatic trance state whereas rabbis and priests, generally speaking, work in ordinary reality. Other reasons for differentiating between the rabbi or priest and the shaman include the fact that the training a priest is required to undergo entails a deliberate course of study of a fixed duration and requires of him no initiatory ordeal such as that experienced by the shaman. "Furthermore, he [the priest] lays claim to no unique, divinely granted gifts and, where the shaman is concerned with the specific human crisis, the priest regards all the crises of life as the result of lapses in the application of an immutable, divinely ordained code" (Rutherford, 1986, p.111). There is also an absence of the hierarchical patterns of social organization found within churches in communities in which shamanism is practised (see Driver, 1991, p.69).

The term "religious formulator" to describe the Baal Shem Tov does not really fit comfortably either though, as was the Bal Shem Tov actually responsible for formulating anything? It can be argued that his recommendations as to how his followers should conduct themselves were in fact passed on to him in other realities by his spirit helpers, and were thus not actually of his own making

"Etymologically, 'religion' comes from the Latin word *'religio'* (*religere*, which literally means 'to tie together again,' i.e., to reunite the creation with the creator)" (Heinze, 1991, p.137). Acting in his / her role as an intermediary, this is what the shaman can be said to do. And it was as an intermediary for others that they traditionally made their living.

Not only can the shaman act as an intermediary between the community he / she represents and the spirits but he / she may also be called on at times to act as a mediator between two members of the community in dispute with each other. And where there is no form of centralized government, in small communities which have no other courts, the séance can provide an effective means of both airing and resolving local conflicts (see Lewis, 2003, p.144).

As intermediary, the shaman can be said to serve as a bridge or a link–"to facilitate the changing of condition without violent social disruptions or an abrupt cessation of individual and collective life"

(Van Gennep, 1977, p.48). Being regarded as an outsider gives the shaman an advantage as it enables him / her "to criticize all structure-bound personae in terms of a moral order binding on all, and also to mediate between all segments or components of the structured system" (Turner, 1995, p.116-117).

By communicating with the spirits on soul journeys and bringing back the lessons he / she learns from them, the shaman has traditionally been able to act as "a curber of other people's crimes" (*cf.* the quote below) and it is in this way that practitioners have been able to regulate the people they represent. Of course it was not only shamans who performed this role but other religious leaders such as the Baal Shem Tov did too. We are told, for example, that

> Every Sabbath, the Baal Shem Tov made a soul-ascent, either during prayer (usually during the *Shemoneh Esreh* of the *Musaf* service), or during his Sabbath afternoon nap, or during a meal – often the third Sabbath meal. Then, at the conclusion of the Sabbath, he went to his room, lit his pipe and, while smoking, revealed to his disciples what he had seen in the upper worlds (Buxbaum, 2005, p.287).

This very much mirrors the way in which indigenous shamans would present their assembled audiences with accounts of their journeys into non-ordinary reality upon the completion of their séances. Also, as was generally the case with the indigenous shaman, the Jewish mystic would face a barrier between the two worlds that needed to be crossed in order to make a soul ascent.

> In performing acts of sorcery, the Jewish shaman traverses the ôøâæã *par'gawd*, the veil of Illusion that separates the spirit realm from the physical realm. It is only an illusion,

because in actuality there is no separation. The veil is in essence the mindset known as *mocheen d'kat'nus*, or finite Mind, the boundaries of givens and definitions that limit our capacity for possibility. Transcending beyond the *par'gawd* the shaman accesses the mindset known as *mocheen d'gadlus*, or Infinite Mind, where everything is possible (Winkler, 2003, p.93).

As James observed, whatever deity the prophets, seers, and devotees bore witness to was worth something to them personally because they could use him. "He guided their imagination, warranted their hopes, and controlled their will–or else they required him as a safeguard against the demon and a curber of other people's crimes. In any case, they chose him for the value of the fruits he seemed to them to yield" (James, 1982, p.329).

Incidentally, we are told that as a seer, the Baal Shem Tov, like many of the shamans of old, was also able to see events happening from afar. "He was not limited by space or time. His physical sight extended to an area of four hundred miles by four hundred miles. His spiritual sight was unlimited – from one end of the world to the other. He saw the future and heard heavenly proclamations" (Buxbaum, 2005, p.227).

In his / her role as an intermediary, the shaman can be seen to be responsible for maintaining the balance of the community and for "creating the harmony from which life springs" (Halifax, 1991, p.15). The Desana payé (shaman) provides a good example of just how this can work in practice:

> The Tukano, one fratrie (kin group) of which are the Desana, number around 7,000. They live in scattered dwellings along the rivers and small streams weaving through the vast

equatorial rain forests of the northwest Amazon. In this little-explored region of the upper Amazon basin, the traditions of the various Tukano peoples have remained more or less intact. The Desana payé ... is the intellectual of his culture as well as a priest and healer. One of the shaman's main activities, however, is establishing contact with the Master of the Game Animals, who controls the success of hunting efforts and therefore the source of food. The payé is a mediator and moderator between the spirit elements that govern the field of life and the social network that is vulnerable to supernatural forces (Halifax, 1991, pp.137-138).

Lewis cites the example of the shamans among the Krekore Shona of the Zambesi Valley, who deal with the moral order and also with the relations of man to earth:

> Disputes are taken to him [the shaman] for settlement, as well as to the official secular courts, and he is also asked to decide issues concerning succession to chieftaincy and quarrels between neighbouring chiefs. In these matters it is the judgement of the guardian spirit, very properly sensitive to public opinion, that is delivered by the shaman (Lewis, 2003, p.123).

Not only Besht, but his father before him too, is said to have spent a significant part of his life apart from the people he served, in the same way that an indigenous shaman would do during his period of apprenticeship: Rabbi Eliezer 'left the city and took up his abode in the wooded forest' (Hilsenrad, 1967, p.15). And only after passing three tests of strength, and when Rabbi Eliezer and his wife were both close to one hundred years old, were they 'blessed with a son, whom they named Yisroel' (Hilsenrad, 1967, p.21). So Rabbi Eliezer was tested before being acknowledged as a holy man in the same way as his son would be one day. Once again, we find parallels with the training of a shaman, in that the three tests of strength that Hilsenrad describes, and Rabbi Eliezer was required to face, mirror the kind of initiation that the shaman was traditionally required to undergo.

As for Besht himself, we are told that while he was still an infant, 'When he heard anyone studying Torah, his face would glow in keenest delight. He gravitated towards good people, and avoided the evil and the false. An unpleasant event in town provoked tears; but each time his mother helped a poor man with food or money, he would laugh in sheer joy' (Hilsenrad, 1967, p.23). All this marks him out from an extremely early age as being different from all the others, as those who were one day destined to be shamans were traditionally found to have been too. Further evidence to support this assumption can be found in the following quote:

"there were occasions when Yisroel would suddenly burst into tears without any discernable cause ... he would often suddenly disappear from town for days; just as suddenly, he would reappear and give no answer to his Rebbe's questions as to where he had been ... sensed from the world of nature, that every blade of grass and every leaf grows and lives" (Hilsenrad, 1967, p.26).

Additionally, as with shamans, there is evidence that Besht had the support of spirit helpers, the old man he supposedly met in the forest who led him to Reb Meir, for example:

'Yisroel immediately sensed that his new mentor was no ordinary man, but a Tzaddik, a profound Torah scholar and perhaps even one of the thirty-six Tzaddikim in whose merit the world exists, but of whom the world is unaware ... The Baal Shem Tov was fourteen years old when he became a full-fledged member of these Tzaddikim Nistarim (secret society of the saintly)' (Hilsenrad, 1967, p.26).

As for Reb Meir, Besht can be said to have undergone an apprenticeship with him. The society of hidden Tzaddikim was

a movement of mystics who rejected the aloof attitude of a religious establishment that focused on the external aspect of Torah scholarship and religion and looked down on the uneducated and imperfectly observant simple people. ... Instead they "taught simple working Jews the basics of Judaism with an emphasis on *musar* (character development and ethics)" (Buxbaum, 2005, p.13).

The hidden Tzaddikim also sought to "enter heaven while alive" [in the same way Elijah the Prophet is said to have done] – to experience godly reality during their lifetime – by means of a fiery devotion to the mystic path" (Buxbaum, 2005, p.29). As for Elijah the Prophet, he is said to have first revealed himself to Israel on his sixteenth birthday. We are informed that from then on "the angelic prophet appeared to the Baal Shem Tov regularly and became his foremost teacher" (Buxbaum, 2005, p.30).

One of the many achievements of the Baal Shem Tov was to reform the approach of preaching of the hidden tzaddikim so that instead of using threats of punishment in the afterlife and descriptions of the terrible suffering in hell to frighten people into repenting their sins, they learnt how to encourage the people rather than rebuke them, as they had previously done.

There is evidence to indicate that being in a trancelike state was something that Besht was familiar with too: 'he would daven in the tradition of Rabbenu Yitzchok Luria, the ARI HaKadosh, for the purpose of achieving a closeness to God through Dvaikus and Hislahavus, i.e., clinging to God amidst fervor and a glowing ecstasy' (Hilsenrad, 1967, p.29).

Further evidence can be found in a letter Besht wrote to Rabbi Avraham Gershon Kitover:

> On Rosh Hashanah of the year 5507 (1746 C.E.), I made a (kabbalistic) oath and elevated my soul in the manner known to you. I saw wondrous things in a vision, the like of which I had never witnessed since the day my mind first began to awaken. The things which I saw and learned when I ascended there would be impossible to communicate, even if I could speak to you in person (Sears, 1997, p.212).

In an alternative version of the 'Holy Epistle' letter that the Baal Shem Tov wrote circa 1752 to his brother-in-law, Gershon of Kutów, which was published in 1971 by Mordecai Bauminger on the basis of a manuscript he claimed was an autograph (written by the Besht's son-in-law and signed by the Besht himself), Besht recounts two occasions when his soul rose up to Paradise, both of which happened on Rosh Hashanah. Together with Yom Kippur (on which another ascent was later reported to have occurred in 5518), "these are the most numinous days in the Jewish calendar, fraught with spiritual tension, when concentrated communication with the Divine is most possible and most likely to be efficacious (Rosman, 1996, p.109). In all three cases known to us, the Besht played the role of shaman, venturing into the spiritual realm to defend his community, or the people of Israel in general. His report of what happened gave the etiology of events that were occurring in real life, provided comfort to survivors, and guided belief and behaviour (Rosman, 1996, p.110).

When asked by his student, R. Adam's son, about how to become worthy, his answer was

> "By undertaking for a period of time to refrain from eating, drinking or yielding to the human weaknesses to which the body falls prey. Then will our souls rise to such lofty heights that they will make contact and communicate with the angel whose domain is the Torah and its secrets. But I warn you there is moral danger in this course. As the soul mingles with the celestial beings and comes closer to its Divine source, it sometimes cleaves to it and refuses to return to this lower existence."(Hilsenrad, 1967, p.41).

What we learn of here is that Besht did subject himself to ascetic practices during his period of initiation, and also that he was aware of the eristic nature of such spiritual practices.

There is also evidence to indicate that Besht was in communication with a sacred teacher in non-ordinary reality for ten years of his life:

> 'In a letter to his disciple, R. Yaakov Yosef HaKohen of Pulnoh, ...the Besht wrote that on the eighteenth day of Elul, 5484, the day he became twenty-six years old the prophet Achiyah of Shiloh [the prophet who lived at the time of David, King of Israel] appeared to him. They started to study Bereishis. And when they had finished the last verse in Devorim, precisely ten years had passed' (Hilsenrad, 1967, p.43).

What we can see from all this is that the Baal Shem Tov, though now regarded as the founder of Chasidus, had exactly the kind of upbringing an indigenous shaman would have had, and that this no doubt helps to account for the special qualities that he possessed that made such an indelible impression on those he ministered to. And this is how 'at the age of thirty-six, in the year 5494 (1734 C.E.), a great new dazzling light burst upon the world. The Baal Shem Tov settled in the city of Mezshbozh, where he began to live and teach the doctrines of Chasidus in public (Hilsenrad, 1967, p.44).

It has been suggested that the main constituents of shamanism are the ability of the shaman to make contact with the supernatural world, to act as an intermediary between those he / she represents and the supernaturals, to receive inspiration from spirit helpers, and to have ecstatic experiences. However, in practice, the shaman's duties depend on specific cultural context and these will clearly vary according to time and place. For example, urban shamans in the 21st century clearly have to adapt to the circumstances in which they find themselves in order to ensure both their relevance and their survival, just as the Baal Shem Tov can be said to have adapted to the times and communities he found himself in the 18th century.

If we now attempt to separate the man from the myth, contrary to what the legends about him suggest, we have to conclude that "the Besht was much more a representative and perpetuator of existing religious, social, political, and even economic realities than he was an innovator" (Rosman, 1996, p.174), and he was certainly no founder of any new movement during his lifetime. "This was the age of popular mysticism in Poland. Holy men whose vocation was magical security were an accepted, normative type in both Jewish and Christian culture. Such a person could attain a respected place and even share in the religious leadership of the community, functioning parallel to the rabbi, who handled ritual and legal matters" (Rosman, 1996, p.175).

What he can be said to have done, though, is to make some significant changes to old-style Hasidism.

> These include attachment to the letters of the texts as an alternative technique for spiritualizing study and the rejection of ascetism as a tool of communion. These innovations had important ramifications for the popularization of Hasidism as an approach to life ... Without the physical commitment required to carry out fasts and flagellations, the kabbalisitc doctrines and rituals were much more accessible. Second, if the significant component of the study texts is the letters rather than the words, then one need not be a sage to have access to the import of these texts. With mystical contemplation, rather than content mastery, as the key to meaningful utilization of the holy texts, the scholar loses his unique status (Rosman, 1996, p.183).

This meant that study of the Kabbalah was no longer reserved exclusively for a chosen few, but open to everyone. In the same way as the anthropologist Michael Harner has made the practice of shamanic journeying available to everyone in our own times, the Baal Shem Tov can be said to have achieved something similar in his own lifetime by helping to change the way Hasidism was viewed and practised.

After considering in some detail the attributes of both the Baal Shem Tov and the traditional shaman, we are left with the question of what makes such people and of how to account for the special gifts they are endowed with. Studies by McClenon in 1994 and Targ, Schlitz & Irwin in 2000

> indicate a constellation of psychological variables that imply the existence of a shamanic syndrome characterized by hypnotisability, dissociative ability, propensity for anomalous experience, fantasy proneness, temporal-lobe signs (measured by questionnaire items regarding unusual experiences associated with temporal lobe epilepsy), temporal lobe lability (measured by EEG), and thinness of cognitive boundaries (measured by Ernest Hartmann's boundary questionnaire) (McClenon, 2002, p.134).

Like many others before him and no doubt like many others who will follow, McClenon goes to great pains to find an explanation for the shaman's special gifts, unable just to accept them for what they are, as an "insider" would be able to do, and thus unable to derive maximum benefit from the practitioner's skills and knowledge.

As to the veracity of the tales reputedly told by, and about, the Baal Shem Tov, "There is no sure way to tell in every case which stories are historically true and which legendary, yet certain stories present a character so original and unique that one is almost certain that they couldn't have been fabricated" (Buxbaum, 2005, p.361). In any case, regardless of whether the stories are true or not, they are also frequently examples of what Jürgen Kremer, transpersonal psychologist and spiritual practitioner, called "tales of power" after one of Carlos Castaneda's novels. He defines such texts as 'conscious verbal constructions based on numinous experiences in non-ordinary reality, "which guide individuals and help them to integrate the spiritual, mythical, or archetypal aspects of their internal and external experience in unique, meaningful, and fulfilling ways" (Kremer, 1988, p.192). In other words, they are tales that can be used for teaching purposes, which helps to explain why they have withstood the test of time so well.

# Bibliography

Buxbaum, Y. (2005) *The Light and Fire of the Baal Shem Tov*, New York: Continuum.

Berman, M. (2007) *The Nature of Shamanism and the Shamanic Story*, Newcastle: Cambridge Scholars Publishing.

Braun, W. & McCutcheon, R.T. (eds.) (2000) *Guide to the Study of Religion*, London: Cassell.

Bulgakova, T.D. (2009) 'From Drums to Frying Pans, from Party Membership card to "Magic Branch" *Withe*: Three Generations of Nanai Shamans' In *Folklore 41* www.folklore.ee/folklore

Driver, T.F. (1991) *The Magic of Ritual*, New York: Harper Collins Publishers.

Durkheim, É. (2001) *The Elementary Forms of Religious Life*, Oxford: Oxford University Press (originally published in 1912).

Edsman, C.M. (ed.) (1967) *Studies in Shamanism*, Stockholm: Almqvist & Wiksell.

Eliade, M. (1989) *Shamanism: Archaic techniques of ecstasy*, London: Arkana (published in the USA by Pantheon Books, 1964).

—. M. (2003) *Rites and Symbols of Initiation*, Putnam, Connecticut: Spring Publications (originally published by Harper Bros., New York, 1958).

Halifax, J. (1991) *Shamanic Voices*, London: Arkana (first published in 1979).

Harner, M. (1990 3rd Edition) *The Way of the Shaman*, Harper & Row (first published by Harper & Row in 1980).

Heinze, R.I., (1991) *Shamans of the 20th Century*, New York: Irvington Publishers, Inc.

Hilsenrad, Z. A.(1967) *The Baal Shem Tov: His Birth and Early Childhood*, Brooklyn, N.Y. Kehot Publications Society.

Hultkrantz, A. (1979) *The Religions of the American Indians*, Berkeley: California.

James, W. (1982) *The Varieties of Religious Experience*, Harmondsworth Middlesex: Penguin Books Ltd. (first published in the United States of America by Longmans, Green, and Co., 1902).

Kremer, J.W. (1988) 'Shamanic Tales as Ways of Personal Empowerment.' In Gary Doore (ed.) *Shaman's Path: Healing, Personal Growth and Empowerment*, Boston, Massachusetts: Shambhala Publications. Pp.189-199.

Lewis, (2003 3rd Edition) *Ecstatic Religion: a study of shamanism and spirit possession*, London: Routledge (first published 1971 by Penguin Books).

Maddox, J. L. (2003) *Shamans and Shamanism*, Dover Publications Inc.

(originally published in 1923 by the Macmillan Company, New York, under the title *The Medicine Man: A Sociological Study of the Character and Evolution of Shamanism*).

Mathews, F. (1994) *The Ecological Self*, London: Routledge.

McClenon, J., (2002) *Wondrous Healing: Shamanism, Human Evolution, and the Origin of Religion*, Illinois: Northern Illinois University Press / Dekalb.

Moscati, S. (1957) *Ancient Semitic Civilization*, London: Elek Books.

Ripinsky-Naxon, M. (1993) *The Nature of Shamanism*, Albany: State University of New York Press.

Rosman, M. (1996) *Founder of Hasidism: A Quest for the Historical Baal Shem Tov*, Berkeley: University of California Press.

Rutherford, W. (1986) *Shamanism: the foundations of magic*,

Wellingborough Northamptonshire: The Aquarian Press.

Sears, D. (1997) *The Path of the Baal Shem Tov: Early Chasidic Teachings and Customs*, Northvale, New Jersey: Jason Aronson Inc.

Shulman, Y.D. (1993) *The Chambers of the Palace: Teachings of Rabbi Nachman of Bratslav*, Northvale, New Jersey: Jason Aronson Inc.

Turner, V. (1995) *The Ritual Process: Structure and Anti-Structure*, Chicago, Illinois: Aldine Publishing Company (first published in 1969).

Van Gennep, A. (1977) *The Rites of Passage*, London: Routledge and Keegan Paul (original work published in 1909).

Vitebsky, P. (2001) *The Shaman*, London: Duncan Baird (first published in Great

Britain in 1995 by Macmillan Reference Books).

Walsh, R. N. (1990) *The Spirit of Shamanism*, London: Mandala.

Winkler, G. (2003) *Magic of the Ordinary: Recovering the Shamanic in Judaism*, Berkeley, California: North Atlantic Books.

# Notes

1. Bulgakova is referring here to the practices of the Nanai indigenous people. The Nanai (*nanaitsy* in Russian) are a people inhabiting the banks of the Amur River (Khabarovsk Krai, Russia) and its subsidiaries of the Ussuri River (Primorsk krai, Russia). A small group of Nanai also live in China, between the rivers Sungari and Ussuri. As for a *withe*, it is a shamanic requisite that is believed to indicate the condition of the patient's energy.

2. It is probably best to discount this biographical detail: "[T]he tradition that he received the mystical writings teaching him the Kabbalistic secrets from Rabbi Adam Ba'al Shem, who lived in the sixteenth century, seems to be an obvious attempt to legitimate the Besht to a potentially doubting public by

placing him under the aegis of a famous, established predecessor" (Rosman, 1996, p.179).

3   This is very much an exaggeration. Students attached themselves to him and certain rabbinical luminaries gave him their support, but not, during his own lifetime, to the extent suggested here. We now know from Polish sources that "during his entire tenure in Mi?dzybó?, the Besht lived tax-free in a house belonging to the kahal that was reserved for public religious figures. He had a recognized, publicly supported role to play in the community and fit comfortably into the existing institutional structure. Those who were closest to him as disciples – Wolf Kuces and David Purkes – were also part of an established communal institution, the bet midrash, while the members of his extended household were identified, and presumably viewed in a positive light, by virtue of their association with him (Rosman, 1996, p.169). It would therefore seem that the suggestion there was a great deal of opposition to the Baal Shem Tov is more than likely off the mark too.

# See also:

## Wanton Green: Contemporary Pagan writings on Place

Edited by Gordon Maclellan & Susan Cross
ISBN 978-1-906958-29-9,
222pp £11.99 / $23

As our relationship with the world unravels and needs to take a new form, *The Wanton Green* presents a collection of inspiring, provoking and engaging essays by modern pagans about their own deep, passionate and wanton relationships with the earth. "Where do we locate the sacred? In a place, a meeting, memory, a momentary glimpse? The Wanton Green provides no easy answers and instead, offers a multitude of perspectives on how our relationships with the earth, the sacred, the world through which we move are forged and remade." Phil Hine.

*Contents*: Foreword (Graham Harvey) ,"She said: 'You have to lose your way'"(Maria van Daalen), Fumbling in the landscape (Runic John), Finding the space, finding the words (Rufus Harrington),Stone in my bones (Sarah Males), A Heathen in place: working with Mugwort (Robert Wallis),Wild, wild water (Lou Hart), Facing the waves (Gordon MacLellan),The dragon waters of place: a journey to the source (Susan Greenwood), Catching the Rainbow Lizard (Maria van Daalen), The rite to roam (Julian Vayne), Places of Power (Jan Fries), Natural magic is art (Greg Humphries), Pagan Ecology: on our perception of nature, ancestry and home (Emma Restall Orr), Because we have no imagination, (Susan Cross), The crossroads of perception,

(Shani Oates), Devon, Faeries and me, (Woody Fox), Lud's Church, (Gordon MacLellan), Places of spirit and spirits of place: of Fairy and other folk, and my Cumbrian bones (Melissa Montgomery), A life in the woods: protest site paganism, (Adrian Harris) We first met in the north, (Barry Patterson), Museum or Mausoleum (Mogg Morgan), Hills of the ancestors, townscapes of artisans (Jenny Blain), Smoke and mirrors (Stephen Grasso), America (Maria van Daalen), Standing at the crossroads, Meet the authors .

mandrake.uk.net
PO Box 250, Oxford, OX1 1AP (UK)
Phone: 01865 243671

CPSIA information can be obtained at www.ICGtesting.com
Printed in the USA
LVOW132217161212

311921LV00002B/29/P